Miss Dreamsville and the Collier County Women's Literary Society

This Large Print Book carries the
Seal of Approval of N.A.V.H.

MISS DREAMSVILLE AND THE COLLIER COUNTY WOMEN'S LITERARY SOCIETY

AMY HILL HEARTH

THORNDIKE PRESS
A part of Gale, Cengage Learning

GALE
CENGAGE Learning

Detroit • New York • San Francisco • New Haven, Conn • Waterville, Maine • London

Copyright © 2012 by Amy Hill Hearth.
Thorndike Press, a part of Gale, Cengage Learning.

Thorndike Press® Large Print Basic.
The text of this Large Print edition is unabridged.
Other aspects of the book may vary from the original edition.
Set in 16 pt. Plantin.

LIBRARY OF CONGRESS CATALOGING-IN-PUBLICATION DATA

Hearth, Amy Hill, 1958–
    Miss Dreamsville and the Collier County Women's Literary Society / by Amy Hill Hearth.
        p. cm. — (Thorndike Press large print basic)
        ISBN 978-1-4104-5407-2 (hardcover) — ISBN 1-4104-5407-X (hardcover)
    1. Life change events—Fiction. 2. Literature—Societies, etc.—Fiction.
    3. Florida—Intellectual life—Fiction. 4. Large type books. I. Title.
    PS3608.E274M57 2013
    813'.6—dc23   2012037256

Published in 2013 by arrangement with Atria Books, a division of Simon & Schuster, Inc.

Printed in the United States of America
1 2 3 4 5 6 7 17 16 15 14 13

For Blair, my husband
and true companion

ONE

My name is Dora Witherspoon but most folks know me as the Turtle Lady. A long time ago, I rescued a snapping turtle the size of a truck tire from the middle of Highway 41, a move deemed so foolish it became local legend. I can't say I'm partial to it, but here in the South, nicknames stick like bottomland mud.

I'd like to tell you a story from my younger days. I've been a storyteller my whole life, but I wasn't ready to tell this one until now. It happened fifty years ago — in 1962. Parts of it are hard for me to share, but the fact is that I'm old now — eighty years of age, if you must know — and probably running out of time. I want young'uns to know about my time and place, the people I knew, and a world that's all but gone. I want them to know that one person can come along and change your life, and that being a misfit, as I was, doesn't mean you won't find friends and your place in the world.

Her name was Jackie Hart, and the first time I set eyes on her was across the counter at the post office. She'd moved to Collier County with her husband and kids from, of all places, Boston. Before we knew it, she turned things upside down faster than you can say "Yankee carpetbagger."

From the get-go, Jackie was a trouble-maker in the eyes of the town fathers, but to the few of us who gave her a chance, her arrival in town was a godsend. She started a little reading group, bringing together the most unlikely people in town, including me. We were all outcasts, but as a group we became strong.

None of us saw these changes coming, though. Jackie was like a late-afternoon storm on the Gulf, the kind that comes from nowhere and sends even the old-time fishermen hurrying to shore. She was a surprise, that's for sure.

I'd been working at the post office for about a year, since my divorce, and there were days — like the one when I met Jackie — that were so slow, I swear I could've watched my fingernails grow if I'd had a mind to. By two o'clock there wasn't a thing to do but watch the horseflies dodge the slats of the ceiling fan. I wasn't supposed to, but I started reading magazines that hadn't been sorted yet. First I studied Mr. Freeland's copy of *Time* magazine. But then I couldn't resist peeking at *Vogue.* No one got *Vogue.* Whoever the person was — a Mrs. J. Hart — was new in town. The rest of the Hart family didn't get much mail, but I had already noticed that Mrs. J. Hart got all kinds of stuff that had probably never — until now — passed through the sorting station up at Fort Myers. *The New Yorker. National Geographic* (generally frowned upon since it might include pictures of naked African people). And, of course, *Vogue.*

I kept returning to *Vogue.* I'm not sure I'd ever seen a copy. I was studying the clothes and models and perfume ads, and breaking post office regulation number 3651 (reading a customer's periodical), when I heard a polite little cough and looked up. And there was Jackie.

She was wearing an enormous straw hat and a pair of sunglasses that made her look like she'd just left a party hosted by Sophia Loren on the French Riviera. Her skin was very white, as if she'd never encountered a single ray of sun, and her hair, peeking out from under her hat, was what my mama

9

would have called "the barn's on fire" red. Add to it the way she carried herself and the result was something we rarely saw in Collier County — glamour.

No doubt about it, she was the most interesting person to show up at my postal counter since Mrs. Bailey White was finally let out of jail and moved back home the year before. While the peculiar Mrs. Bailey White was a curiosity, the stunning woman now standing before me was something else entirely. You could be sure she'd never been called mousy, a word I often thought of in connection with myself. I felt like a hick in my humble seersucker dress with the self-tie belt, and was glad she couldn't see my penny loafers. She had what Mama called an hourglass figure, which made my flat little chest and rear end seem positively boyish in comparison.

"Oh, is that the new copy of *Vogue*?" she asked, with an innocence that might have been phony but I wasn't sure. She spun the magazine around and examined the cover.

"Hm," she said. "I do believe this is my copy."

I would have died of shame except I wanted to see what she would do next. Yet all she did was stand absolutely still, waiting for me to answer.

"Yes, ma'am," I said, and my voice came out kind of hushed. "I'm very sorry. I admit I was violating post office regulations. Please," I added, "don't tell my boss or I could lose my job."

She took off her sunglasses and looked at me, eyeball to eyeball. Her eyes were large and round and skillfully made up. "I would *never* do that," she said, adding, "but in the future, could I read my magazine first, please? And then you can borrow it when I'm done? Would that be all right?" Everything came out as a question.

I was pretty sure — but not 100 percent — that she wasn't being sarcastic. I pulled together the rest of her mail and gave it to her. She walked to the door, then stopped. Looking back at me, she asked, "What else do you like to read?"

I couldn't have been more surprised if she'd asked for directions to the nearest pool hall. "Well, um, sometimes I read *Life* magazine," I said. "And *Ladies' Home Journal*."

"Do you like novels?"

I shrugged my shoulders. "I haven't read too many."

"Well, once I am settled, I am thinking of asking the library to start a women's reading group. I was thinking we could call it

11

the Collier County Women's Literary Society. Would you like to be part of it?"

"Well . . . okay." I was not really sure I meant it, although a part of me was deeply flattered.

"What, may I ask, is your name?"

"Dora," I said. "Dora Witherspoon."

Less than a month later, I started seeing flyers around town announcing the first meeting. "A women's literary society — what the hell is that?" my boss, Marty, muttered. Jackie had posted a flyer on the post office bulletin board, next to the Collier County mosquito spraying schedule and the pulled pork fund-raiser that the Masons made everyone suffer through every year.

"It's just people who like to read books," I said.

"You mean like the Bible?"

"I don't know. Maybe cookbooks. Maybe a few novels."

"Novels?" Marty raised an eyebrow.

"Well, how much trouble can we get in, reading books at the library?" I said, a little irritated. "As a matter of fact, I may go myself." Marty could be condescending, and he was convinced everything was a plot hatched by Communists.

"Oh, I guess you're right," he said finally.

Now I felt like I had to go. Besides, maybe

I would learn something new. I wasn't what you'd call worldly. In fact, I'd never been out of Florida. But I'd had two years at the junior college in Saint Petersburg, and while it was just a hundred and twenty miles up the Gulf, the experience had been an eye-opener. One of my professors was from Nevada. Another, from New Orleans. My fellow lodgers at the rooming house where I lived were women who had either retired to Saint Petersburg or (in the case of one lady, whose story I never learned) seemed to be running away from something up north. From them I learned about places like Ohio and Pennsylvania. There was one lady, a Mrs. Jamesway, who had a subscription to a big-city newspaper called the *Toledo Blade*. Even though it arrived in the mail three or four days after it was published, it was still fun to read.

After I finished junior college, I married Darryl and moved to Ocala. That's horse country, in north-central Florida. Like me, Darryl was from Collier County — I'd known him my whole life. But while I was at school, he started a small construction company and somehow got a job building a gorgeous new estate near Ocala for some rich folks from Kentucky. The barns Darryl built were nicer than any house I'd ever

13

been in. The owners — a man and his wife in their fifties — talked about impossibly wonderful places they traveled to often, like London, New York, and San Francisco.

Any dreams I had for the future ended with my divorce. My parents were dead, I'm an only child, and I was inching up on my thirtieth birthday. I had nowhere else to go except the little cottage in Naples that had been in my father's family for three generations and was spitting distance from the Gulf. I needed a job, but the only person who would hire me was my cousin Marty, who ran the post office. Everyone else treated me like I had mange.

I didn't have high hopes when I went to the first meeting of the Collier County Women's Literary Society. To my surprise, seven people showed up, which was five more than I expected. We sat on folding chairs in a little circle — Jackie, me, Miss Lansbury (the librarian), Mrs. Bailey White (the old lady who had returned from jail the previous year and was always called by her entire name as a sign of respect for her age), a young colored girl wearing a formal maid's uniform, a woman in her fifties who wrote poetry and said her name was Plain Jane, and the town's one and only Sears employee, Robbie-Lee Simpson, Collier County's only obvious homosexual.

Miss Lansbury spoke first. "Welcome!" she said in her brisk, pleasant librarian voice. She wore a sleeveless sheath in pale green with a floral-patterned scarf that was perfectly matched. I tried to guess her age and concluded she was probably about thirty-five. She was still considered new in town — having lived here only ten years or so — and suspiciously single. However, seeing as she was a librarian, people let it go. After all, she was that rare bird — a career girl — and destined to be an old maid, a problem of her own making. She had beautiful black hair thanks to her Spanish ancestors. "Mrs. Jacqueline Hart" — she gestured politely toward Jackie — "who just moved to town from Boston, has spearheaded this new group. Mrs. Hart, would you like to tell us a little more about yourself?"

Jackie looked surprised but rose to the occasion. "Well, my family moved here exactly one month ago. My husband, Ted, is the new business manager for the Toomb family. We have three children — twin girls who are fourteen and a son who is twelve."

She didn't have to explain who the Toomb family was. They were one of the most powerful families in South Florida, though a rung or two down from the Colliers.

Everyone had heard that old Mr. Toomb, who wanted a better grasp of how things worked in the North, had gone out and hired a business manager from Boston. The man he hired was Ted Hart, a World War Two Army veteran who had put himself through college on the GI Bill.

"Oh," Jackie added, "and please call me Jackie."

"You mean like the Jackie in the White House?" Mrs. Bailey White asked lightly.

"Well, not quite like her, no," Jackie said and smiled. "I have a northern accent, that's true. But I'm not skinny and I couldn't hope to be as elegant as *that* Jackie."

But the comparison, in one way, was striking. I couldn't imagine Jackie Kennedy *or* Jackie Hart adapting very easily to life in our little town. People think of Naples as one of the richest, swankiest places on earth, but back in 1962 it was a sunbaked southern backwater no bigger than a cow pie. There were maybe eight hundred people living here, a number that grew to a whopping twelve hundred or so in the winter when the Yankees would come down to fish for sea bass and snook. Naples was a redneck town and proud of it.

I have to admit that moving here was a pretty raw deal. I say that even though I'm

16

from Collier County and have at least a smidgen of pride. But relocating here must have been especially shocking to Jackie. She was, clearly, a "Boston girl" through and through. Cultured. Progressive. All that Yankee stuff we Southerners find so irritating.

No one knew what to say next, so Miss Lansbury jumped in again. "Well, I must say I am delighted. Thrilled. I think the rest of us know who each other are, right? Oh, one more thing: Robbie-Lee, this is supposed to be a women's literary society, so you shouldn't really be here. But if everyone is okay with it, I suppose it's all right. Does anyone have any objections?"

No one did, so Robbie-Lee stayed.

I was actually more surprised that the Negro girl had come. You never saw colored folk at the town library. Her being there was bold, even reckless. Then again, what would we have done to her? Given her the evil eye until she left? Made a fuss and told her to leave? None of the rest of us sitting around our little circle seemed to be looking daggers in her direction. Maybe the Collier County Women's Literary Society would be that rarest of organizations — an integrated one.

I suppose it's still basically true, but in

those days, white people tended to fall into three categories. There were those who went out of their way to harm or hold back Negroes in any way they could. Then there were those who never gave Negroes much thought and really didn't care. And then there was a small group of white folks who felt badly about the cruel way Negroes were treated and wanted to see things improve.

I was raised to be in the last category. My father, who I don't remember well, was said to be a regular old redneck. But Mama was a nurse, and during her training someone had drilled into her head that all people were human and should be treated accordingly. She worked for the only doctor in town, and sometimes, when she was needed at the four-bed hospital, she would treat colored folks who came to the back door. But she didn't advertise that she did this and told me to keep quiet too. Strange to think you could get hurt because you'd been helping someone.

Mostly, though, I'd had little interaction with Negroes. We lived in different parts of town and belonged to different churches. The Supreme Court of the USA had famously decided, back in the fifties, that schools were supposed to be integrated, but here in Collier County they apparently

hadn't gotten the message. The white kids were still picked up by a shiny yellow school bus and taken to their well-kept schools — grammar, junior high, and a new high school north of town. The colored kids were picked up by a bus that predated World War Two and looked like it had survived (more or less) Hurricane Donna. The so-called colored bus went in the opposite direction, to a single school — first through twelfth grades. I had never been there — I don't think any white person ever had — but I heard the place was a shambles.

Now, if my family had been rich, we would have had colored servants, but Mama, being a widowed nurse with little money to spare, did her own cooking, cleaning, and ironing. Same with everyone else in our part of town. We'd see Negroes now and then, but they didn't talk to you and you didn't talk to them. I thought they were the unfriendliest people on earth. Only when I was older did I realize they were avoiding us to stay alive.

As we sat around the little circle with Miss Lansbury as our leader, I tried not to stare at the colored girl. I wondered what she would do about the curfew (eight p.m. in the summer, six p.m. in the winter, when nightfall came earlier), which applied only to Negroes. But she herself brought up the topic. "My name is Priscilla Harmon and I would like to be part of this group." She had taken off her maid's cap and perched a pair of horn-rimmed glasses on her nose. She looked like an entirely different person. "I love to read," she added. We all nodded and smiled. Encouraged, she said, "I would like to go to college, maybe Bethune-Cookman."

"Oh, that's marvelous!" Jackie said. "What would you like to study?"

"Well, I would . . . I would like to be a teacher. Maybe an English teacher."

I tried to hide my astonishment. I wondered how realistic this was. I knew the answer — not very.

"My only problem," Priscilla was saying, "is that if you all are kind enough to let me belong to the group, I will need a ride home — you know, on account of the curfew." She ended with a sweet, hopeful smile that revealed the most beautiful teeth I ever saw. They were the same color as the starched white collar that framed her face.

"Well, of course we'll take you home, dear," Jackie said. "It's not a —"

"You may have to take me home too," Robbie-Lee interrupted. "I don't stay out after dark either." This was a stunning admission, and the closest Robbie-Lee had ever been (as far as I knew) to acknowledging his homosexuality.

"Well, someone may have to take me home too!" We all turned and looked at the petite Mrs. Bailey White. She had a loud, authoritative voice when she needed to.

"Oh, why is that, Mrs. Bailey White?" Miss Lansbury asked. "Are you not driving anymore?"

"I'm not allowed to have a driver's license. That's part of my parole deal."

This was quite a conversation stopper, and the rest of us fidgeted in our hard metal chairs until Miss Lansbury — thank the Lord — took the lead again.

"Well, I am sure we can take care of these *transportation issues*," she said, emphasizing the last two words. Miss Lansbury had a way of making every little thing sound important. Maybe that's something they teach at librarian school.

"May I speak for a moment?" Jackie asked, raising her hand like a schoolgirl. "I want to explain that what I have in mind is a salon."

"You mean like a beauty parlor?" Robbie-Lee asked.

"No, dear, not that kind of salon," Jackie said. "There was a time when a *salon* meant a gathering of people who discussed the issues of the day. They would meet in the parlor of someone's huge, oversized house and discuss literature, art, politics."

"I have a huge, oversized house," said Mrs. Bailey White. It wasn't really an invitation but more like a statement of fact. Still, even the suggestion of meeting at her place gave me the creepy-crawlies, since she had gone to prison for murdering her husband in that very house. I wasn't sure if Jackie knew of Mrs. Bailey White's checkered past, but she must have picked up on the uneasiness that swept through the rest of us like a rogue wind off the Gulf.

"Well, that's very nice," Jackie said politely. "Perhaps someday you will be kind enough to have us over."

"But does this mean we're not going to read books?" asked Robbie-Lee, still a little confused.

"Yes, we will read books," Jackie replied patiently. "We will be centered around books. But I am suggesting we choose books that make us think and expand our horizons. If we read a book about music, we might invite a musician to perform as part of our book discussion. The idea is to read books that stimulate our minds and challenge us to think about the issues of the day."

We responded so enthusiastically that we sounded like an amen chorus.

"But if you'll permit me to say so," Jackie continued, "I am thinking we really must meet here, at the library, as a way of letting the community know that everyone is welcome. This is not a private club."

These words were met with a second round of approval. I felt punch-drunk (not that I've ever actually been punch-drunk in my life, on account of a promise I made to Mama). Private clubs, official and otherwise, were pretty typical in our little town. I looked from face to face around the circle. None of us was Junior League material; none of us had big money; Mrs. Bailey White was an ex-con. If you were colored, homosexual, a divorced postal worker (me), or — God forbid — a sexy redhead with a Boston accent newly arrived in town, you were on your own. But Jackie was suggesting that we form our *own* group. And meeting at the library would give us cover.

A place to belong? Here in Naples? Just the possibility made me giddy as a jaybird. I began feeling something in my heart that I thought was long gone and buried. I'm not 100 percent sure, but it might have been hope.

Two

The worst day of the year, if you worked at the post office, was when the Sears catalogs arrived. Every family in Collier County, and throughout the universe for all I knew, got at least one copy of that darned catalog. Rumor had it you could kill a man if you heaved a Sears catalog at him, or derail a train by placing one strategically on the tracks. They were that big.

The *quietest* day of the year was the day after they were delivered. Kids would choose their clothes for the coming school year — socks, pants, underwear, bathing suits, churchgoing clothes, you name it. Then the moms would figure out what they needed, and when the fathers came home, they'd do the same. Even the women who sewed their own clothes needed something — a girdle, maybe — from the catalog. If you wanted something special — say, a pair of Levi jeans — you had to drive all the way to Maas

Brothers in Fort Myers. Few people had the money to do that, and even among those who did, southern pride kicked in and they stayed home. Going to Maas Brothers to shop meant you were uppity. *Real* Southerners shopped from the Sears catalog, they did without air conditioning even if they could afford it, and they never, ever sunbathed or wore sunglasses.

Once you figured out what you wanted from the catalog, you could fill out a form and mail it to Sears. If you wanted faster service and cheaper shipping, which most of us did, you could go to the Sears Service Center. This was not actually a store but a place that resembled a hamburger stand. The one employee for the past five or so years was Robbie-Lee Simpson, the man who had joined our Women's Literary Society, a move that was either brave or bizarre, depending on your point of view. Robbie-Lee's job was to "expedite" (his word) your order, whatever that might be. He had, however, shown a special talent for home décor and had developed a loyal following of customers, all women. My own mama had gone to him for advice on ordering curtains. She'd had big plans to redecorate but died before she could finish the job.

Right smack in the middle of Sears catalog

25

week — when the end was in sight but my boss, Marty, was tired and cranky — two things happened at the exact same moment that could have cost me my job. A boy about fourteen years old brought an injured snapping turtle — wrapped in a tarp — right into the post office and asked for my help. And with uncanny timing, my ex-husband, Darryl, showed up and made a scene about how I should be a good wife and move back to Ocala with him.

I was in back with the turtle, which was ripping a hole in the tarp, when I heard Darryl's voice. "Dora, I need to talk to you," he said in a tone that made me think he'd been drinking.

The turtle got loose and started moving around underneath the mail-sorting table. The boy had a deep scratch on his left arm already. "You go on home," I said. "I'll take it from here. And thanks for bringing him in."

"Dora, you need to come to your senses and move back home with me," Darryl was pleading.

"And you need to get the hell out of here!" This from Marty, who had just walked in on this pretty scene. Marty had never liked Darryl much in the first place. "This is my post office! Now get out!"

"This is not *your* post office," Darryl yelled back. "It belongs to the United States Government!"

"Why don't the two of you shut up and help me," I said. Darryl walked out, but Marty, bless his scared little heart, crouched down and together we pressed our hands firmly on the turtle's back to keep him steady.

"You see the problem?" I said to Marty. The turtle had a long crack in its shell. We were basically holding the shell together.

"Wow, he's a goner," Marty said.

"No," I said. "Just hang onto him." I left poor Marty there alone but returned as fast as I could with a roll of duct tape.

"Aw, come on, you dumb critter, I am saving your life," I said to the turtle. I taped the crack while Marty watched, shaking his head. When I was done, we both jumped back, and I chased the turtle into the restroom and closed the door tightly.

"Don't worry, I'll take him home later," I said to Marty. "They calm down after a while."

I already had three turtles convalescing at my little house — Norma Jean, Myrtle, and Castro. Sometimes they never left, just lived by the little pond in my yard. Norma Jean was the largest one and very territorial. I'd had Norma Jean for years. Norma Jean had even gone to Ocala with me when I got married. Darryl — and I give him credit for this — didn't seem to mind. Sometimes Norma Jean made a noise that resembled a dog barking. Darryl said instead of a watchdog, I had a watchturtle.

"You know, with all this turtle stuff, maybe you were lucky to get Darryl in the first place," Marty said, catching his breath. "If he's willing to put up with that, maybe you ought to go back to him."

I didn't say a thing. I'd felt enough pressure already to go back to Darryl. Women didn't leave their husbands. They just didn't.

With Marty's help (and part of a hamburger one of the guys had dumped in the trash) I coaxed my new turtle — I decided to call him Marty — into the rolling cart we used for unloading the mail truck. Once the turtle was in the cart, he settled down long enough for me to get him home. I kept him separate from the others, feeding him sardines (a treat) in a pen I built myself just for this purpose.

The days crawled by, there was no more sign of Darryl, and Marty (the turtle) was doing nicely. The next meeting of the literary society was coming up, and I realized I was looking forward to it with an eagerness that made me feel slightly pathetic. We had finished our first meeting without deciding what book we were going to read — not a great start, I'd say, for a literary society. But as Jackie had said, we were more than that. We were a *salon.*

We had agreed to meet weekly. (At least we agreed on that.) Jackie would drive. The only one who didn't need a ride was Miss Lansbury, who owned a small Volvo. Plain Jane, we realized, lived catty-corner to Jackie, so she would be picked up first. I was next.

When the day arrived, I waited in front of the post office complex, as everyone called the butt-ugly building where I worked. To my way of thinking, the word *complex* was such an overstatement, it made the building seem even smaller. In truth, the complex was just one building with three tenants: the Rexall Pharmacy, the Book Nook (mostly magazines and paperbacks), and the post office, the last being the smallest of the three — so tiny, in fact, that if the name of our town had been any longer, it wouldn't have fit on the sign.

Waiting there, and looking out at my humble little town, I thought of something Jackie said at the end of our first meeting. When they arrived here, Jackie had tried to get the kids excited about their new hometown, so she took them for a drive. She was trying to stay upbeat for all of their sakes, but then she spied Big Bert, Ernie Sanders's hound dog, sleeping in the middle of the road. Big Bert was old and didn't hear too well. We were used to driving around Big Bert, but Jackie, of course, was caught by surprise. She hit the brakes and her car stopped maybe twenty feet from that fool dog. Jackie said Big Bert lifted his head and sniffed. Then he rolled over, rubbed his back in the dirt, yawned, and continued his little siesta. Jackie admitted that she'd thrown the car in park and cried right then and there. This was just off Fifth Avenue, the main road through town. The way she told the story, she seemed to find it funny — after the fact, anyway. But I could surely see her point. She was a long way from Boston.

Standing in front of the so-called complex, I broke one of the time-honored rules for proper southern ladies: I leaned against the building. For some reason this act was associated with pure laziness or something truly wicked, maybe even prostitution. At the moment, I was so hot and tired, I didn't much care.

While I'd been living up in Ocala, somebody got the brilliant idea to add an outdoor clock and temperature gauge at the bank, directly across from where I stood. The clock tended to be slow or would stop altogether, an annoyance to most people, but to me, it seemed like a message that time had passed me by. As for the temperature gauge, well, no one needed to be reminded that it was hot outside. In fact, some folks in town believed, as I did, that it was better not to know at all, and the exact temperature was a subject best avoided.

By now I was truly tired of waiting. I considered walking to the library, but it had been built north of the new high school and would be too far in the heat. Finally I went into the Rexall, sat at the counter, and ordered a root beer float and a grilled cheese sandwich. By the time Jackie pulled up and tapped the horn twice — assuming, correctly, that I'd emerge from the building — I almost had a handle on my grumpiness.

Jackie's station wagon looked freshly washed, no small accomplishment when you drive mostly on unpaved roads. I climbed into the backseat and fought the urge to stretch out and go to sleep. But with the windows rolled down, I began to feel something close to human once the car moved forward.

We were on our way to pick up Priscilla at the house where she worked. When we pulled into the drive, I was surprised by the size of the house, which was completely hidden from the road. It was a stucco mansion, probably built in the 1920s, and the kind of place that reminded me that I was dirt poor.

These people were rich — maybe not stinking rich but pretty close. People in Collier County with money were few and far between, and their deep pockets usually had something to do with large-scale agriculture. They might own a place out in the sticks, like a plantation, and a separate house in Naples, which they considered "in town" because there was a doctor, a bank, and the post office. I had a vague recollection that the lady of this house was a distant member of the Toomb family. I'd seen the name in the social pages, back when I'd bothered to read them. The Toombs seemed to ooze money. Even the far-flung relatives had money to burn. I began to wish I'd just stayed home, but as it turned out, I was needed.

Jackie made an awful mistake, one that only a Yankee would make. She pulled up close to the front door, threw the car in park, and hopped out.

I called after her. Jackie should have stayed in the car and waited for Priscilla to come out, but she sashayed — plain as day — right up to the front door and knocked.

Priscilla answered. Just as I feared, the white lady Priscilla worked for must've made a beeline for the foyer, 'cause suddenly she was looming over Priscilla's shoulder.

"Priscilla, are you ready?" Jackie asked gaily. "Oh, hello there," she added when she saw the Boss Lady. Jackie was so loud we could hear her from inside the car. Plain Jane shrank in her seat but I couldn't help but look. Priscilla was wide-eyed, and Boss Lady glowered like a junkyard dog. As for Jackie, her smile melted faster than ice cubes on asphalt. She knew she'd messed up. But she was totally confused, as any Yankee would be.

"Ready? Ready to go *where?*" Boss Lady said finally, her lower jaw sticking out. In a daintier woman, her expression would have seemed like a pout.

Priscilla sputtered, and Jackie spoke up. "Why, we're on our way to the library."

"The *library?*" Boss Lady moved forward. She looked from Jackie to Priscilla and back again, finally fixing her gaze on Priscilla. "Why would you be going to the *library?*"

33

Priscilla gave Jackie a warning look. Suddenly, Jackie understood. Boss Lady didn't know Priscilla could read. That she liked to read. That she had a life of her own and maybe even a future.

It must have gone against every bone in Jackie's body, but she was willing to be a jerk if she could save Priscilla's job. "Why, Priscilla here is helping us at the library, aren't you, dear? She's a volunteer — isn't that wonderful? I bet she didn't even tell you. Of course, she doesn't do anything *important* — she just waits on us hand and foot, pretty much like I'm sure she does here. She makes the coffee and cleans up afterward, and sometimes she even cleans the toilets."

This last bit of sarcasm soared right past Boss Lady, who nodded and tried a small smile. "Oh, I see," she said. "Well, Priscilla, you are full of surprises. But doing your civic duty is important."

"Yes, ma'am," Priscilla said flatly. Then she gave Jackie a "don't you dare go any further" look.

In the car, Priscilla waited until Jackie pulled away. Then she lit into her.

"How could you do that to me?" she wailed. "You upset Mrs. B and you had no right. I *need* that job!"

I was definitely on Priscilla's side. While I didn't always find the nerve to stand up for myself, I could be downright feisty when I thought someone else had been "done wrong," as Mama used to say.

"What were you thinking?" I snapped at Jackie. "You can't play games with people like Priscilla's boss! Priscilla will end up paying the price! Don't you understand that?"

I gave Priscilla a clean hankie. Priscilla was only about ten years younger, but I felt almost maternal with her sitting there sniffling and all hunkered down in the seat.

I could see part of Jackie's face reflected in the rearview mirror. She seemed to be in shock and fighting back tears herself. Plain Jane pretended to look out the window; Jackie clutched the wheel and drove slowly, the car barely moving. Priscilla stopped crying and closed her eyes.

Jackie suddenly pulled the car to the side of the road. She turned toward the backseat. "Priscilla, I apologize," she said.

Priscilla hesitated. She opened her eyes and nodded, accepting the apology gracefully. But I wondered if Priscilla would continue with our group after that night. I didn't think so.

"Maybe next time we can pick you up

somewhere else," I said to Priscilla. "How do you usually get home after work?"

"I walk to the corner of Vine and Picayune and wait for the bus," Priscilla said, "though sometimes I stay overnight here, if they need me. But I don't really like to." There was no energy in her voice now.

"Well, maybe next time we can pick you up at the bus stop," I said soothingly.

"Yes," Priscilla said, "that would be fine." She smiled at me shyly.

Except for Jackie's occasional questions about directions, no one said much while we traveled to our next stop, Mrs. Bailey White's house. I didn't think we would ever get there. As the crow flies, Mrs. Bailey White didn't live that far from Priscilla's boss, but the house was at the end of a private driveway that was at least a quarter mile long and was lined on both sides with spindly, sickly looking pine trees. Finally we passed some outbuildings — maybe, at one time, a carriage house and a barn — that told us we were nearing Mrs. Bailey White's house. We were a long way from nowhere, and it was a little unnerving, but at least the mood in the car had changed.

When the house came into view, Jackie hit the brakes so hard, we slid to a stop. It was the scariest-looking place I ever saw, and evidently Jackie felt the same.

"My!" Jackie said, speaking for all of us.

"Let's go home," Plain Jane said.

"We can't! We have to pick up Mrs. Bailey White," Jackie insisted. We started moving forward again. Very slowly.

I babbled nervously. "Do we really want her in our group? Maybe we don't need her in the group."

"What exactly happened here?" Jackie whispered.

"No one knows the whole story," I said, "but she killed her husband back in the twenties."

"How did she do it?" Jackie asked.

"Do what?" Plain Jane said.

"Kill him?"

"Poison," I said. "No — wait — I think she shot him. There was a rumor she used a twelve-gauge with both barrels but she seems awfully tiny to pull that off. So I would guess she used a pistol."

"Seriously?" Even Jackie seemed to be losing her nerve now.

Priscilla surprised us by speaking up calmly. "Well, whatever happened, she served her time. They let her out of Lowell and sent her home, so I think we have to give her a chance, just like the Lord would. We should forgive."

"My goodness, Priscilla," said Jackie, her voice full of admiration. "You are the youngest one here and you are leading the way! And you are so right." She hit the gas and the car lurched forward.

I was almost afraid to look at the house too closely as we came near. After all, this was a murder house, and as every good Southerner knows, it's better not to come eyeball to eyeball with a murder house. Everyone knows that a ghost will leave you alone if you keep your prying eyes to yourself. But everyone else in the car was gawking, so I figured I might be able to get away with a quick look.

The house was a tall, shabby, three-and-a-half-story Victorian. I wasn't sure if it was a Queen Anne or a Queen Whatever, 'cause I never could get that straight. The house was wood that, at one time, might have been painted white. To have a wood-sided house in South Florida, you either have to be very rich or very crazy. Since the house was still standing and maybe a hundred years old, my guess was cypress wood. Most of the windows were boarded up. There was a huge vine — hopefully, not poison ivy — climbing up one side and lurking over most of the roof. You get a vine like that around here, the darn thing will grab hold and crush your house. It's only a matter of time.

Mrs. Bailey White must've been sitting on the veranda, just out of sight, because she popped into view, waving so enthusiastically that we all winced with shame. Truth be told, when she clambered down the steps, I was relieved, since I had no desire to leave the car and knock on that door.

Priscilla bravely scooched over closer to me, making space for Mrs. Bailey White. With the bright light of day shining on her face, Mrs. Bailey White looked her age, which was probably around eighty, give or take a few summers. Being a tiny little thing — she reminded me of a sandpiper — Mrs. Bailey White had a bit of a tug of war with the car door. I was just about to get out and help her when she yanked the door open with a burst of strength that was a little scary. She greeted us with a broad smile, and as she settled into the seat, the distinct odor of mothballs hung in the air.

"It's been a long time since anyone's been by here," she said. "Well, other than the grocery boy who leaves my order on the bottom step. But he's gone like a jackrabbit."

I bet. That's what went through my head. And probably everyone else's.

"I know the house doesn't look too good,

but I'm working on it," Mrs. Bailey White added cheerfully. She was wearing the same little pink suit, at least twenty years out of date, that she'd worn before, and her stockings sagged a little around her ankles. "It's hard to get workmen out here. And when they're here, they're terribly disruptive. So I'm just taking things a little at a time. Right now I'm almost done with the parlor."

"Hon," I said, "maybe you need to get some more work done on the outside. I'm a little worried about that vine there."

"Oh, I know," she said. "But I've only been back home for eleven months and three days. And as they say, Rome wasn't built in a day. I had to board it up before I left, and all my money was frozen while I was gone, so there wasn't much I could do."

"No one bothered the house while you were gone?" Priscilla asked politely.

"Not at all! Everyone was too scared to go near the place."

Jackie changed the subject. We had gotten to the main road. "I am lost!" she said. "All turned around! Someone tell me how to find Robbie-Lee from here, please."

The Sears Service Center was plunked down in the middle of nowhere, yet in a spectacular example of overkill, the out-of-town builder had included a paved parking lot and, incredibly, sidewalks. This had led to rumors that one day there would be an actual store there, but no one really knew one way or the other.

Robbie-Lee was waiting outside, drinking a Coke and half-reclined on a small bench. Seeing us, he polished off the Coke and jumped to his feet with the slow-motion grace of a gazelle. With his Ray-Bans, pressed chinos, and short-sleeved shirt, he looked just like Rock Hudson or some other California movie star, especially when he tossed his sports coat over one shoulder and walked smoothly our way.

The only room left was up front. Plain Jane slid over toward Jackie, and Robbie-Lee climbed in. "Hello, ladies!" he sang out, so cheerfully and warmly that the sound of his voice (not to mention the sight of him) put a temporary end to our uneasiness over Mrs. Bailey White's past.

Robbie-Lee was what my mama's generation called "a doll" — handsome, charming, debonair, and absolutely useless in the romance department. "Are we ready, ladies?" he asked, as if we were headed to a Hollywood red-carpet gathering. Jackie laughed and put the car in gear. I knew what she was thinking — what we were all thinking. He wasn't interested in any of us, not in the biblical sense. But sometimes it was awful nice to have a man along for the ride.

THREE

We decided our first book should be something challenging, just so no one in town would be able to say we were a bunch of lightweights. I'm sure Jackie had all kinds of ideas, but she insisted Miss Lansbury make the first selection. Miss Lansbury chose a book by Rachel Carson called *Silent Spring.*

None of us ever looked at the poor Everglades the same again. We'd been raised to think of nature as our enemy. But as we learned from *Silent Spring,* you couldn't drain the swamps, or use DDT to kill mosquitoes, without a reckoning. The eggs laid by some birds were becoming so fragile — because of DDT — that they'd break under the weight of their mothers' tiny bodies. One day soon, if we didn't stop, we might wake up to the sound of nothing — no birds singing. A silent spring.

We were stunned by the book. Jackie wrote a letter to the newspaper, begging parents to keep their children indoors with the windows closed when the DDT mosquito-spraying trucks passed through their neighborhood. One day I saw kids chasing the trucks on their bikes, darting in and out of the DDT fog. This made me so crazy, I ran after them, yelling, until they stopped.

"It's poison," I said, out of breath.

"It is not," one boy said defiantly. "It's just fog."

"It's a *chemical*," I said. "You shouldn't be breathing that stuff. Think about it." After that, I didn't see them chase the DDT trucks anymore.

Although we all felt passionate about the book, Miss Lansbury reacted the strongest. She talked to some of the local fishermen and learned they'd already noticed that fish in the canals and ponds had not been biting like they used to: fewer mosquitoes meant fewer fish. She wrote letters and sent them to the governor and the state legislature. Although she didn't hear back, she kept trying. She even included some God-fearing scripture about the dangers of mankind's arrogance, thinking that might get through to the old boys in Tallahassee.

We spent a couple of weeks on *Silent Spring*. Since we were a salon, and not just a literary society, someone suggested we invite Mr. James T. Rahway to demonstrate the art of beekeeping.

Mr. Rahway was a man in his eighties who was considered a little peculiar on account of his extraordinary devotion to bees. He brought his little traveling display and gave a talk called "Without the Brilliant Honey Bee, We Are Toast."

"I am spreading the gospel," he told our little group, and for a moment I thought we were about to be evangelized. "The gospel," he added, seeing our confusion, "according to Nature." He then went on to explain all about bee pollination and how, without bees, we would eventually have no plants to eat.

Mr. Rahway made a huge impression on us, though to be honest, Miss Lansbury was not having a good night. She seemed eager to get the bees out of her library.

Then we had to move on. Robbie-Lee wanted to know if we could show a movie, but there was concern all around that we'd upset the owner of the only theater in town. *Theater* was, frankly, a grand name for what was really an old Army Quonset hut, the most terrifying place on earth during an electric storm on account of its being made completely out of sheet metal. Still, the

Quonset hut was enormously popular and locally famous as the first building south of Fort Myers to be air-conditioned. Miss Lansbury said she was not sure if the library could show a movie anyway, except for someone's home movies, which didn't sound too appealing.

So the discussion veered back to books. Mrs. Bailey White was interested in mysteries and true crime. I don't know if it was the topic or because she's the one who made the suggestion, but nobody was taken with the idea.

Miss Lansbury tossed out the idea of reading *Profiles in Courage* by John F. Kennedy, who, after all, was our president. A good choice, you might think, and yet no one was particularly enthused.

"I know what that book's about," Jackie said with a sniff. "It's about eight men who showed great courage at some point in their lives. Why is it always men? He couldn't find any women who showed great courage? That annoys me."

"No Negroes either," added Priscilla.

"That's because the book's about eight US *senators,* and there aren't any Negroes," Mrs. Bailey White said. "And not too many women, for that matter."

"That is beside the point!" Jackie exclaimed. "By focusing on the status quo, he perpetuated the idea that courage is something found only in white men."

"Well, the book won a Pulitzer Prize for History," said Plain Jane.

Jackie was really on a tear. "Of course that book won a Pulitzer Prize! That's the type of book that always wins! Look at who chooses the Pulitzer Prizes! Why aren't there more books about women, or by women, that win?"

"Actually, quite a few women won the Pulitzer Prize — in the fiction category, at least," Miss Lansbury replied in her authoritarian voice. "In the nineteen thirties, especially. But through the nineteen forties — after Ellen Glasgow won in 1942 — the winners were men until Harper Lee won last year for *Mockingbird*."

"So there was an almost-twenty-year stretch when only men wrote novels worthy of the top prize in the country?" Jackie said bitterly. "When I was in high school, we weren't assigned to read any books by women. I went to the city library, and some nice librarian introduced me to Jane Austen and the Brontë sisters, otherwise I wouldn't have known about them."

"Why does it matter?" Robbie-Lee asked.

Our heads swiveled in his direction like a

47

bunch of voodoo dolls. Poor Robbie-Lee.

"It matters because women are different from men, and we have different experiences than men," Jackie said icily.

"Oh," Robbie-Lee said miserably.

"A book by a woman speaks to women," she added, trying to get through to him. "When I read Laura Ingalls Wilder and the Nancy Drew books as a little girl, I could relate in a special way. Same thing with *A Tree Grows in Brooklyn*."

"I thought you grew up in Boston," Mrs. Bailey White said.

"Yes, Boston," Jackie said, thrown for a moment. "What, do you think because I lived in Boston, I couldn't read *A Tree Grows in Brooklyn*?"

"I don't know what I meant," Mrs. Bailey White conceded. "I'm just not used to having conversations like this."

This discussion was sinking faster than a Yankee trying to traverse Blue Heron Creek in hip waders. Robbie-Lee made an end run around the subject by suggesting we try something light. "How about a book about Grace Kelly?" he asked, looking from one face to another around the circle, hoping for a consensus. Robbie-Lee was obsessed with Hollywood. The book he had in mind was called something like *Princess Grace:*

The Woman. The Actress. The Legend.

Plain Jane countered by putting serious poetry on the table. She suggested something by an up-and-coming poet, someone named Sylvia Plath. I had not yet figured out Plain Jane at all. Her accent did not place her as a local. She spoke little of herself, leaving few clues in ordinary conversation. And I was surprised that any woman would accept being called Plain Jane. Heck, it was worse than the Turtle Lady. And she wasn't even all that plain. Nondescript, maybe, with gray hair and gray eyes, and a wardrobe of A-line skirts and blouses with Peter Pan collars. But not exactly plain.

I was so lost in these thoughts, I was shocked when Jackie turned to me and asked, "What about you, dear? What do you think?"

Well, I wasn't accustomed to people asking me what I think. In fact, I'm not sure anyone had ever posed that question to me before, at least not so directly. I could be outspoken, like when I scolded Jackie for putting Priscilla in a bad spot. But I was pretty gutless about my own opinions.

"You mean, which of these books do I think we should read next?" My voice sounded squeaky, like a cartoon character's.

"No, I meant, what book would you suggest?" Jackie said, giving me an encouraging smile.

I couldn't think of anything other than *To Kill a Mockingbird,* probably because Miss Lansbury had just mentioned it. I said the title apologetically and added, "Of course we've all read that."

Hands up around our little circle showed I was right — everyone had. "Well, let's think of another southern woman writer," Jackie said.

"Eudora Welty!" I said with newfound confidence. "My mom named me after her. My full name is Eudora Welty Witherspoon."

Jackie gasped, which startled all of us. "Your mother named you after an author?"

"Well, yes," I said, adding, "is that good or bad?"

"It isn't good *or* bad! It is *magnificent!*" To our amazement, Jackie pulled a handkerchief from her purse and began to dab her eyes.

"And where is this incredible mother of yours now? Wouldn't she like to join our group?"

The others looked at me sadly. "Well, Mama died," I said. "She's buried at the Cemetery of Hope and Salvation, the one that's flooded all the time. Near the Esso station on the Tamiami Trail. You know where that is?"

"Well, no," Jackie said. "I'm sorry, Dora." We were all silent for a moment until Jackie added, "Did she tell you *why* she named you after Eudora Welty? I assume she was your mother's favorite writer."

"Yes, Mama loved her writing. But there was more to it than that. They knew each other somehow. My mother was raised here in Florida, but her people came from Jackson, Mississippi."

"Really! How fascinating! Now tell us, which is your favorite Eudora Welty story?" Jackie said, while everyone else stared.

I felt my cheeks burning. "Well, I haven't really read many of them. I started reading one about a bridegroom when I was about thirteen, but I thought it was kind of peculiar. So I didn't finish it."

Miss Lansbury spoke up. "You must mean *The Robber Bridegroom.* That particular book is a little fantastical for most people's taste." We agreed to let Miss Lansbury research all of the Welty books and make a recommendation.

We were about to wrap up when Jackie said she had an announcement. We had been meeting on Wednesdays, when most of the town was at Baptist evening services and would leave us alone. But Jackie asked if we could switch to Tuesdays. "The reason is — I have a job!" she said proudly.

A *job?* White, middle-class, married women didn't have jobs. Unless, of course, they fell on hard times, like me, after my divorce. White women joined Junior League or volunteered at church. They went to lunch. They baked pies. Some of them played tennis.

"My kids are in school, my husband is busy, and I am not going to let my mind rot!" Jackie declared. "But don't worry, I will always have time for our salons."

In a way it was a relief, because we all could see that Jackie didn't have quite enough to do. A few weeks before, she had come up with this idea she was going to learn how to fish. She went down to the old fishing pier with a hat and sunglasses, looking like Ava Gardner. She watched the old-timers until she was ready to try. But when she hooked a stingray, and the scary beast yanked the pole from her hands, she lost her nerve.

Then she started going to the flower-arranging club run by Miss Beulah Babcock. But this ended in disaster when her last-minute entry to the annual flower show was picked by out-of-town judges as "best arrangement." The other women — especially Beulah Babcock — couldn't live with the fact that a Yankee carpetbagger with a big bosom and red hair had walked off with the most coveted prize.

"Well, what kind of job did you get?" Mrs. Bailey White asked. She had disbelief, and maybe a pinch of envy, written on her face.

"I am going to be a part-time copy editor at the *Naples Star*," she said, referring to the local newspaper.

"What's a copy editor?" Robbie-Lee asked.

"Oh, just a person who reads the stories and edits them and fixes the typos, checks the spelling, things like that," Jackie said.

"How did you come across this . . . job?" Plain Jane asked.

"Well, I wrote a letter to the editor of the paper — remember that? The one about children playing in the DDT fog? And the editor called and asked me to stop by. You know him? Mr. Tarleton. He said my letter was well written and that he needed someone to help out on the editing desk. I said yes without even thinking."

"Your husband doesn't mind?" Mrs. Bailey White asked. Just her saying the word *husband* made several of us cringe slightly.

"He has no say in the matter," Jackie

replied firmly.

"I want to find a husband like that some-day," Priscilla said softly.

"Well, I don't know if you want one just like Ted," Jackie said crossly. "He's on the road all the time with his new job. He doesn't pay enough attention to me, and neither do my darn kids. My son drives me crazy — he has this idea he's going to be a *minister* someday! I don't know who put that idea in his head. When he's not blowing up the carport with his chemistry set, he's read-ing the Bible! And my daughters — the twins — I won't bore you to death about them. They don't do anything but fight. I thought twins were supposed to get along! I love my kids. But I should have waited. I should have finished college, maybe gone to law school. I had applied to go back to school when Ted accepted this new job, and we had to move. And naturally, I wasn't even consulted."

We were stunned by her honesty. None of us could look her in the eye. Women were supposed to get married and have children and feel blessed about the whole arrange-ment. Sure, there were some unhappy women, but they didn't *talk* about it. They just drank too much or got a little too friendly with someone else's husband.

Those who'd never married were regarded as tragic old maids. I noticed the pity they had to endure, along with a rude assumption that they had time on their hands. The most unappreciated chores were foisted on them, like planting petunias beneath the "Welcome to Naples" sign. If you were divorced, like me, that was far worse. You were a failure. A failure as a woman and a human being. No matter what the circumstances, the divorce had to have been your fault. Women were supposed to stand by their man, even if he turned out to be the biggest jackass south of Tallahassee.

We all just sat there, uncomfortable that Jackie was unhappy, and — more to the point — that she had shared her true feelings. None of us was raised to have this conversation.

Mrs. Bailey White broke the silence. "I still think we should read a mystery or maybe some true crime." Turning to Miss Lansbury, she asked, "Is there a book on how to find someone?"

The rest of us exchanged glances. Find someone? Find who? "Well, I'll look into it," Miss Lansbury said with a professional air.

Robbie-Lee had a talent for knowing when to change the subject. "Wait a minute! Why not read *Breakfast at Tiffany's?* We've all seen the movie! I bet most of us haven't read the book! And then we can compare the book and the movie. What do you say?"

His enthusiasm won the day. He had pulled a switcheroo on Mrs. Bailey White's weird ideas, but even better, he had diverted Jackie from making any more embarrassing confessions about her life. If there was one thing that made us flinch, it was a Yankee who didn't understand that we not only don't discuss our private business, we don't want to hear about anyone else's either. And yet Jackie's tirade was, well, kind of *liberating* to hear. I had lived my whole life around people who were expert at the art of disguising their true selves. We always thought Northerners lacked manners and good taste. What they considered an admirable trait — being "direct" — just seemed like rudeness to us.

But I saw that this directness, or whatever you wanted to call it, was not necessarily a bad thing. At least with Jackie, you always knew where you stood.

FOUR

Out of all of us in the group — and this surprised me — the two who became close friends, outside our regular meetings, were Jackie and Plain Jane.

Of course, Jackie's house wasn't more than a shout away from Plain Jane's. Their houses faced away from each other on separate streets, but the yards were back-to-back. All you had to do was pick your way through the maze of clotheslines to get from one patio to the other. Before long, Jackie was going over there for a quick cigarette and a highball every evening before she got dinner started for the kids and for Ted, if he wasn't out on the road.

So that is why Jackie learned the real story about Plain Jane long before the rest of us. Plain Jane said she was living on a widow's pension, that her husband had drowned in some kind of fishing accident that was too painful to talk about, and that she spent her days reading poetry and making baby blankets for the maternity ward at the Negro hospital in Fort Myers.

The story about the baby blankets was the only part that was true. Plain Jane had never married and was living in our quiet little backwater because she was a writer living, as they say, *incognito.* A very successful writer.

This is how the secret came out. One day Jackie popped in and Plain Jane was acting a little funny, like she had something to hide, Jackie said. There, sitting on the dining room table, was a stack of typewriter ribbons and at least a dozen reams of paper. Jackie, as usual, got right to the point:

"Are you writing a book?"

"What if I am?" Plain Jane replied.

"Oh my God! You *are* writing a book! What kind of book?"

Plain Jane sat down at the dining room table with a sigh. "This has to remain confidential or I will lose my job," she said.

Jackie would have promised to give up cigarettes, chocolate, and her library card for a year to be brought in on a good secret. I bet she nodded up and down like a bobblehead toy on the back shelf of a Chevy. But when Plain Jane opened her mouth, what she said was the last thing in the world

58

Jackie thought she'd hear. "Well," Plain Jane said, clearing her throat, "I write romance novels. And articles about sex."

Give Jackie credit for taking this in stride. "Well — how exciting!" she said, apparently without a hint of irony.

Jackie said Plain Jane shot her a look and said, "Are you making fun of me?"

"Of course not!" Jackie said. "How completely wonderful! How long have you been doing this?"

"Oh, for years," Plain Jane said. "Years and years."

"And why would you lose your job if people knew?"

"Because if my editors in New York ever found out that I'm a fat, wrinkly fifty-five-year-old lady, they'd dump me in a minute. I mean, look at me, Jackie. I was never great-looking even when I was young! People would expect me to be young and gorgeous."

"Would they? Yes, I suppose they would," Jackie said, answering her own question. "How terribly unfair. I'm forty and fat, so I guess they wouldn't let me write for them either." This thought, no doubt, made Jackie very sad.

"You're not fat, you're plump," Plain Jane told her. "And you're curvy. My editors

59

would accept you better than me. They'd have a heart attack if they saw me."

"And of course, the people around here — well, they'd go crazy," Jackie said, thinking aloud. "You'd have to leave town, I suppose. Tarred and feathered, isn't that the expression?"

Plain Jane winced and folded her hands in her lap. Jackie knew she'd gone too far. "Fear not, my friend, I shall keep your secret," she declared. "Perhaps someday you will tell our reading group. But I have one question for you — how do you maintain this secrecy? Haven't you ever met with your editors in New York?"

"No," Plain Jane said, "they've never met me in person. I have a mysterious *persona*. It's part of my image. I just communicate with them through the mail. I keep a post office box in Miami."

"Brilliant! Simply brilliant! Would you allow me to read something you've written?"

Plain Jane hesitated. "Well, actually, right now I'm working on an article for a new magazine, *Sophisticated Woman.* They asked me to write a piece for them. The market is supposed to be independent-minded, sexually aggressive, gorgeous young gals working in a cosmopolitan setting."

Plain Jane left the room and returned with

a typewritten draft, which she presented to Jackie. "Go ahead," she said with a shrug. "Tell me what you think."

"Should I read aloud?" Jackie asked.

"Whatever you want."

Jackie began to read slowly, articulating each word, starting with the headline. " 'Sex on a Desk: Your Boss's Ultimate Fantasy. And the Best Way to Get That Raise. By Jocelyn Winston.' Jocelyn Winston — that's you?"

Plain Jane nodded her head. "I don't think Jane Wisniewski has quite the same impact, do you? I mean, Jocelyn Winston sounds like someone who might actually have sex on a desk. And Jane Wisniewski doesn't."

"Right," Jackie said, before continuing: " 'What happens behind closed doors in Manhattan after hours? Ask Debbie, a twenty-five-year-old confidential secretary to a powerful Manhattan attorney. "Sex," she says. "That's what's happening. Sex in elevators. Sex on the floor. And sex on a desk. That's what men really want. That's what everyone's doing, all over town." ' "

Jackie looked at Plain Jane. "Sex on a desk? That doesn't sound so great to me. I mean that doesn't sound very comfortable. How did you find out about this? How did you do your research?"

Plain Jane blushed and looked away. "You didn't actually do this, did you?" Jackie said.

"Of course not." Plain Jane sounded annoyed.

"Well, then, who told you about this?"

"No one told me. I made it up."

"Made it up?"

"Sure."

"Do your editors know?"

"Of course not. They think it's real."

"Oh my God." This was a lot for Jackie to take in. "You mean there are no sex-starved females having sex on their desks? With their bosses? In Manhattan?"

Plain Jane shrugged. "Not that I know of."

The two women sat quietly, trying not to look at each other, or at least that's how Plain Jane remembered it later on. Finally, Plain Jane glanced directly at Jackie. A smile was beginning to appear at the corners of Jackie's mouth and got wider and wider until it turned into an ear-to-ear grin. Jackie then made a sound like a hiccup that was, in fact, an attempt at stifling a chuckle. The chuckle finally exploded into a howling, knee-slapping, fist-pounding belly laugh that sent Plain Jane's cat skittering under the couch.

For a fraction of a second, Plain Jane thought Jackie was laughing at her. Then she realized it was more of a "you've got to be kidding, you've fooled the whole world" kind of laugh. Plain Jane started giggling, and before long, the two of them were shrieking and howling loud enough to wake the dead. Then Jackie slipped off her chair, which made them laugh even harder.

They were carrying on so loud, they didn't hear the knock on the door. They didn't notice Jackie's son, Jude, until he'd let himself in and was standing there gaping at them. "Mom, you gotta come home," Jude said, when they finally noticed him. "I burned the pot roast."

"Oh my God, the pot roast!" Jackie shrieked. Then, to Jude: "Did you take it out of the oven?"

Jude looked bone tired. "Of course I took it out of the oven," he said. He was a strange kid, wise and patient and world-weary for someone who was only twelve. He was like a little old man wearing a kid suit. "Mom," he added, "we need to talk."

"Where are the twins? Did they set the table?" Jackie asked.

"No," Jude said. "They haven't done anything. They've been fighting over that stupid curling iron again."

"Well, Jude, is this something you can talk

about right now? Or should we wait till later?"

"Now is okay," he said, glancing at Plain Jane.

Jackie looked pale and serious. "What is it, Jude?"

"Mom, I have to change my name. I can't live here with a name like Jude. All the kids are calling me Judas."

Jackie was quiet for a moment. "Changing your name because other people don't like it is not worthy of you, Jude. Your real friends will accept you, whatever your name is."

"I don't have any real friends." Jude looked really angry. "How could I have any real friends? We just moved here. I hate it. I hate my name. I hate this place. And sometimes, Mom, I even hate you." This last part was said calmly, which was even more chilling.

Jackie's lower lip trembled. "It's normal to hate your mother sometimes, Jude."

"It's your fault we moved here!"

"Are you out of your mind?" Jackie was suddenly angry. "It was your father's idea to move here! You should blame him, not me! Do you think I ever would have left Boston for this place? Don't you know how much I hated moving here? We're in this

64

together, Jude."

"Don't call me Jude."

Jackie cleared her throat like she was trying to calm herself down. "Perhaps what you need is a nickname. Like Skip or Biff or something like that."

Jude scoffed. "Those are northern nicknames, Mom! They're worse than Jude!"

"How about Judd?" said Plain Jane, the first time she'd spoken since Jude arrived. "Judd sounds like a good ol' southern boy."

"It does?" Jude sounded hopeful. "What do you think, Mom?"

"If it makes you feel better, I'm all for it," Jackie said. "Now let's go home and see if we can rescue that pot roast." She stroked his hair, red like hers except for blond streaks from the sun.

I'll say one thing about Jackie. Nobody was ever going to mistake her for one of those sweet, tireless, patient TV moms like June Cleaver on *Leave It to Beaver.* By comparison, she was a catastrophe. But once in a blue moon, she got it right.

FIVE

From the minute we started the Women's Literary Society, people began asking questions. Because I worked at the post office — especially when I was stuck doing counter duty — people grabbed the opportunity to quiz me down. A day didn't go by without a customer asking, "Can I have a four-cent stamp, please? And by the way, what is this Women's Literary Society you belong to?"

They didn't want to join us. They just wanted to know what the heck we were doing.

I felt defensive. I liked my new friends and I didn't feel it was right for people to expect me to defend them or explain why I spent time with them. It was my business. We were a little band of oddballs trying to survive in a time and place where sameness was revered. Because of my divorce, and the mean way I'd been treated, I had more compassion and was more open to different

66

kinds of people. And I had less patience for small-town people who thought they knew everything and wanted to tell everybody else how to live.

Even with the part-time job and our literary society gatherings, I sensed that Jackie was still not happy. I was beginning to worry that one day she'd be up and gone. But then one little event intrigued her. Of all things, what captured her attention was the fall fund-raiser for the Lions Club. For a two-week period each year in Naples, women could walk up and kiss any man, single or married, who grew a beard or mustache. Since the men who kept shaving during those two weeks had to pay a "fine," this meant there were a lot of hairy faces available to be kissed.

Most of the ladies of Naples did not, of course, partake of the opportunity. It was just a game. But then along came Jackie. At last, something about Naples that Jackie could like, and she took full advantage. One of the men she had her eye on happened to be the owner of our one-and-only local radio station, WNOG, "Wonderful Naples on the Gulf." His name was Bill McIntyre, he was in his late twenties, and Jackie had remarked on more than one occasion that he was "Cary Grant cute." She walked right up to him and planted one right on him, almost knocking him over. This happened right under the bank clock. She told us later that his mustache tickled. Anyway, he must not have minded, because after the initial surprise, they ended up having a conversation. He knew she worked part-time at the newspaper, because the *Naples Star* was right next door to his radio station and there was some sharing of information between the two, like calendar items and ad copy. So he had seen her around.

But he had never heard her voice. Suddenly he was all business. "Has anyone ever told you that you have a wonderful voice?"

Jackie thought he was flirting. "Why, yes, they have."

"I mean a wonderful *radio* voice," he said.

"Oh," Jackie said. "No, I don't believe they have."

"Well, you do." Jackie said you could practically see ideas hatching in his brain. "I'm looking for someone to do a late show — midnight to two a.m."

"Is that so?" Jackie asked.

"The show would be taped. You would come into the station anytime and record your intros and voice-overs. My station manager doubles as the sound engineer and he would handle the rest."

"Well, that's a lovely idea, but haven't you noticed my New England accent?"

"It's your voice I'm talking about. If you speak slowly enough, you should be able to hide the accent. Come to the station and we'll do a test."

Jackie liked the sound of that. It seemed glamorous and adventurous.

"Okay," she said. "But what kind of show? Would I be introducing music?"

"Yes, sort of a *Good Night, Naples* show."

"Would I get to pick the music?"

"Sure," he said.

"And could we keep my identity a secret, just to keep people guessing?" If there was one thing Jackie loved, it was intrigue.

"Wow, great idea!" he said. "So the only people who would know are me and the station manager! Now come by the station and let's do that test."

Jackie had to go to the Winn-Dixie to get the fixin's for a birthday dinner for the twins, but she didn't think this was a good image for a budding radio star. "I have an important errand I must do," she said. "How about later, like four o'clock?"

"Make that four thirty, 'cause everyone else will be gone by then."

"Oh," said Jackie. "You mean so we'll have some *privacy.*"

Jackie admitted later that she'd gone too far. That poor young man blushed so hard, he turned purple. "I mean, if we're going to keep your show a *secret,*" he stammered.

"Right," Jackie said. She was beginning to regret the kiss. This needed to be a professional relationship. A ten-minute conversation under the bank clock had turned into an extraordinary opportunity.

Well, four thirty could not come fast enough, and once she was seated in the sound room behind a microphone, she was in her glory. With coaching from her new best friend, Bill, Jackie did her sultry best to ditch the Boston accent.

"It'll get easier, and we can always retape," said the station manager, a wiry fellow with a deep tan who had once served in the Canadian Air Force, where he had learned his trade. Around town he was always referred to as "that guy from Canada who works at the radio station" — or, for short, "Canada" — even though he'd lived in Naples for twenty years or more. Jackie, who could not bring herself to call him Canada, learned that his real name was, in fact, Charles and became the only person in town who used the poor man's given name. Apparently thrilled by this development, Charles took an immediate liking to Jackie.

Since she had already bonded with Bill, she now had the approval of the only two people she needed. The truth is that in a few short hours — somewhere between the bank clock, the aisles of Winn-Dixie, and a stop at home to put food in the fridge and leave a quick note for the kids — she had fallen deeply, desperately in love with the idea of having a radio show.

Since she had passed her audition with flying colors, the rest would come easy. Within a few days she had chosen her theme song, a choral rendition, with full orchestra, of a sentimental Henry Mancini ballad called "Dreamsville." The song was heard frequently on the TV series *Peter Gunn,* a show about a private eye that had gone off the air a year earlier.

Bill and Charles were thrilled. This would be her signature song. They wrote a press release, which was published in the newspaper where Jackie continued to work part-time: "New Show on WNOG to Feature Mystery Temptress."

That last word was Jackie's idea. Bill thought *temptress* might incur the wrath of the Baptists, maybe even the Methodists, but he went along with it. And he started promoting the show like mad.

The launch of a late-night radio show —

one with a hint of honest-to-gosh sex appeal, even — was a thrilling prospect in Naples. Late at night, we couldn't pick up anything except Havana. The only exception was Saturday nights, when we could usually get WSM all the way from Nashville and listen to the Grand Ole Opry.

The first night of the new show, I stayed up and tuned in like everyone else. There were a few seconds of music — the "Dreamsville" song — followed by a woman speaking in a low, sexy voice, each syllable drawn out.

"Hello . . . This is Miss Dreamsville . . . bringing you beautiful music . . . to soothe the soul . . . and lull you to sleep." Like everyone else in Naples, I was racking my brain trying to figure out who in the world was this woman? A few ideas went through my head. Not one of them was Jackie.

I remember the very first songs she played — "Crazy," sung by Patsy Cline, followed by Nat King Cole's "Mona Lisa," and ending with Elvis crooning "I Can't Help Falling in Love with You." Then the woman with the sexy voice came on again. "Did you like that, Naples? . . . Would you like some more?" And so it went, until she signed off at two a.m., saying, "Good night . . . Naples," and a few bars, again, of "Dreamsville."

The next morning, Naples was in an uproar. Every God-fearing soul wanted to know — *had* to know — who Miss Dreamsville was. This was the most exciting thing that had happened since a lifeguard from Everglades City got chewed up by a shark and lived to tell about it. Heck, we'd never had a radio show after midnight, and this was the first time there'd been a woman on the air at WNOG.

At the Edge of Everglades House of Beauty, the proprietor, Bunny Sanders, insisted she had the inside track on figuring out Miss Dreamsville's identity. "I know every woman in this town," she'd say in a loud voice that contradicted her feminine name. "I will be the first to figure this out."

If the women in town were curious, the men were obsessed. Teenaged boys and young unmarried men, especially, were convinced that Miss Dreamsville was drop-dead gorgeous, like Ursula Andress or Raquel Welch. We'd hear them talking all over town: maybe, they'd say, she was a former Swamp Buggy Queen or even a Miss Florida.

Across from the side entrance to the Book Nook was Ray's Barbershop, a tiny building that appeared exactly square, like a sugar cube. Ray's was communications central for the menfolk in town, and when the windows and door were left open — which was nearly all the time — you could hear the men gossip. In the days before air conditioning was common, there were few secrets.

"Oh, that Miss Dreamsville!" one old man would say. "What do you think — blonde or brunette?"

Then another old man would say, "I'd sure love to get my hands on Miss Dreamsville."

And a third voice — maybe the barber's — would say, "Ha! You wouldn't know what to do with a woman like that."

Jackie proved very good at keeping her secret, even from her family. She figured that taping her intros at different times, on different days of the week, would help confuse people. Since she still worked part-time at the newspaper, no one would be suspicious if she was seen near WNOG.

Personally, I was relieved that this mysterious Miss Dreamsville had become the center of attention, rather than our literary society. The questions about what we were reading and why (and always with the assumption that we must be doing something wrong) stopped overnight. All anyone could talk about was Miss Dreamsville, and that was fine with me.

Six

There's an old saying that you don't know diddly about someone unless you've seen where they live. That was certainly true of Mrs. Bailey White and it turned out to be true of Priscilla and Robbie-Lee too.

The first time Jackie drove us all home from our "salon" was an eye-opener. Since Jackie had picked up Priscilla, Robbie-Lee, and me at work, she'd need an entirely different route for dropping us off. It took a good ten minutes for us to figure out an itinerary that made any kind of sense, with Robbie-Lee finally taking out pen and paper and drawing a little map.

We'd already seen where Mrs. Bailey White lived, so dropping her off after dark was nothing new, except her house looked even spookier. Jackie planned to drop off Plain Jane last, of course, since they lived so near each other. I was to be the second-to-last dropped off.

First we drove Priscilla home, then delivered Mrs. Bailey White to her big old house, and finally drove over to Robbie-Lee's neck of the woods. There were no streetlights outside downtown Naples. Jackie made us all lock our doors. She was rattled by a story in the newspaper about Florida panthers making a comeback in the swamps. "Panthers!" she was saying. "Nobody told me about panthers! It's not bad enough we have to worry about alligators."

I didn't want to argue with her, but frankly a panther would not pose a serious threat to people in a station wagon with the windows rolled up tight.

"Personally, I think the rednecks are scarier," Robbie-Lee said, trying to be funny, but somehow his joke fell flat.

Priscilla lived in the old colored section south of town. Some of the Negro population had moved to an area closer to Naples — to a block behind the gas station — into housing called the Quarters. This was a small housing project, promoted by the town fathers as a step up for colored folks. I didn't pay much attention when they were building it, but I remember Mama muttering under her breath. She saw right through it. "Sure, they'll have indoor plumbing," she said, shaking her head. "And they'll have lovely little apartments, and they'll be closer to their jobs." I didn't understand her point until she looked me point-blank in the face and said, "Don't you see? They're going to lose more than they'll gain." Sure enough, soon after the public housing was built, those who'd moved to the housing project lost what little freedom they'd had. A patrol car passed back and forth like a shark, all night long.

But Priscilla lived with the holdouts on a sandy stretch of road about three miles south of Naples. If you were white, you had never visited that area. Yet there we were, piled in Jackie's station wagon, headed to Priscilla's grandma's house and pretending that this was the most normal thing in the world.

The journey was so slow-going, I was beginning to feel like we were driving to Key West. Of course, maybe it just seemed that way. Everyone knows a destination always seems farther when you're trying to get there than when you're coming back. I thought we must be getting close when we came to a sharp bend in the road, but there was nothing there but a pretty little church in a clearing. We drove on, perhaps another half mile, maybe longer, when I began to see a cluster of bungalows tucked here and there among the cypress trees. Unpainted, and built at haphazard angles to one another, they were mostly hidden from the road, even in the glare of headlights from our car.

I had to wonder about Priscilla. She was going against the grain by being with us. Heck, she wasn't legally supposed to be out at night at all. But she seemed completely at ease, telling Jackie to turn left or turn right, until we got to her grandma's bungalow.

"Where are the people?" Robbie-Lee asked. I had noticed the same thing. On such a beautiful night, people should have been sitting outside.

"They're hiding," Priscilla said. "You know — because of us."

"Where shall I park, dear?" Jackie asked, a bit formally. There wasn't anywhere to park a car, and in fact I knew we'd have some difficulty actually turning around.

"This is fine," Priscilla said. "I'll just get out here. Thank you so much for the ride. And thank you for having me in your literary society." She was so sweet and sincere, you just wanted to hug the stuffing out of her.

It took Jackie a good five minutes to turn the car around. As we pulled away from the bungalow community, Robbie-Lee peered out the back window and said, "Look, I think I can see some people." And sure enough, now that we were leaving, we could see outlines of men and women in the moonlight.

"My," Jackie said after a while, "I need a cigarette."

We drove at ten, maybe fifteen miles an hour. A mule could have gotten us home faster. But Jackie was nice enough to give us a ride, so we said nothing. Eventually we were back on familiar turf and, finally, at Mrs. Bailey White's.

Since this was the first time Robbie-Lee had seen Mrs. Bailey White's house, he expressed surprise. "Dang," he said. "That's some house."

Mrs. Bailey White responded with a small smile, which meant who knows what. She must have been tired like the rest of us, 'cause she did not drag out her good-byes. "Thank you, all," she said. "This is the most fun I've had in a long, long time."

I didn't even have the energy to consider what Mrs. Bailey White may or may not have meant, but Plain Jane's actions said it all. She called out, "Good night," and then rolled her window back up so fast, I thought she might break the handle. Somehow I doubted it was panthers she was worried about.

Robbie-Lee, we soon learned, lived deep in the heart of an area known as Gun Rack Village, where the menfolk were partial to shooting at each other. I was surprised Robbie-Lee lived back there, because these were the last kind of people on earth who would tolerate a person who might be a homosexual. The so-called road that brought us to his house was no better than the sandy trail we took to Priscilla's. Of course, this was the exact opposite direction. Jackie was getting one hell of an education, just by driving everyone home. But without a ride, I expect they wouldn't have come; like most people who didn't live in town, they walked a mile or two to a main road and prayed for a bus to come before they got eaten alive by skeeters.

The house where Robbie-Lee lived was a small fishing lodge converted into a home. The place was ablaze with light; in fact, as we came near, we realized there were floodlights pointed at us.

"Ah, Dolores is waiting up for me," he said. "She's always watching my back." This last comment was said with pride.

"Dolores?" asked Plain Jane, thinking what we all were: *Robbie-Lee lived with a*

80

woman?

"I call my mom Dolores," he said. "She never did like it when I called her Mom." Dolores, he added, was retired.

"Retired from what?" asked Jackie.

"She was a dancer in Tampa, pretty successful, but then she had me. She was tired of all that anyway, so we moved down here to get away. I grew up right here" — he pointed to the house and the clearing — "and Dolores makes a good living hunting alligator."

"She hunts . . . alligators," Jackie said. She had trouble just saying the word. "Isn't that illegal? I mean, isn't that . . . poaching?"

Robbie-Lee employed a classic southern technique: he ignored the unpleasant question and just kept talking. "She sells the gator meat at the farmers' market and sells the skins by mail order." From the admiring tone of his voice, you would think his mother ran a tea shop where she sold homemade cookies to lonely war veterans.

"Isn't she afraid of the . . . alligators?" Jackie asked.

"Dolores isn't afraid of anything," Robbie-Lee said cheerfully. "She's got a real talent with a steel-wire lasso. And even though she's lost her looks, the men around here still like her. She's kind of a character."

Now I understood how Robbie-Lee, Naples's only obvious homosexual, was able to survive: no one messed with him on account of his mother.

The station wagon slid a bit on the sand as we pulled up to the doorstep. "It's a lot like driving on snow," Jackie marveled. "I think I can get the hang of this."

Robbie-Lee took Jackie's hand and kissed it, a gesture that could not have seemed more out of place. "Good night, ladies," he called to us. I didn't even look toward the house as he went in; the blinding floodlights made that impossible. But at least we knew he'd get safely inside. Dolores would see to that.

By the time we got to my house, all I wanted to do was drag my exhausted self inside. I wondered about these new friends of mine and hoped I hadn't gotten in over my head. I had a funny feeling they were either going to drive me nuts or become the best group of friends I'd have in my whole life. As things turned out, it was a little of both.

SEVEN

We were still reading *Breakfast at Tiffany's*. The film starring Audrey Hepburn had come out the previous year and — as Robbie-Lee had predicted — we'd all seen the movie, except for Mrs. Bailey White, because she'd still been at the state women's prison at Lowell.

"You know, this book is about a call girl. You might not guess that from watching the movie," Jackie complained.

"She's not a call girl," Robbie-Lee said. He looked offended.

"Well then, how is she making a living?" Jackie demanded.

"She's a New York café society girl," Robbie-Lee countered. This was like a tennis match. The rest of us looked back and forth as the two of them took turns.

"Aw, come on, she makes a living by getting money from rich old men," Jackie said. This was getting ugly.

"Well, I don't see it that way," Robbie-Lee said. "She was just charming and young and funny and men liked to spend time with her."

"Ugh," sniffed Jackie.

"Well, the movie does not really follow the book that closely, wouldn't you agree?" This was Miss Lansbury, using her librarian's voice to get them back on track.

"Well, I wish I had read the book first, because I couldn't see Holly Golightly in any way, shape, or form other than Audrey Hepburn." This from Jackie, who still had her nose out of joint.

"She was magnificent," Robbie-Lee said. It was amazing how much he admired women, considering he had no carnal interest in us whatsoever.

"Everyone loves Audrey Hepburn," Plain Jane said, putting her two cents' worth in. Priscilla nodded sweetly in agreement.

"Yes, and she's so cute and adorable, there's no way you could believe that the character is, uh, a call girl," said Robbie-Lee. "I mean, it's not about sex."

"Yes, it is about sex!" Jackie cried. "It's implied throughout the movie! The character is pathetic, when you think about it — a young, beautiful catastrophe. Why do they have to portray women like that?"

"Who?" asked Mrs. Bailey White.

"Hollywood," said Miss Lansbury.

"And male writers. Like Truman Capote," added Jackie.

I was glad no one expected me to say anything. It's not like we went around the circle and everyone had to chime in. I noticed Plain Jane had an interesting technique — raising questions instead of giving her opinion. I decided, then and there, that I ought to learn how to do it. "But don't you love reading about New York, about people who move in those circles?" Plain Jane asked.

"Well, sure," Jackie said.

"I had trouble imagining the Holly Golightly character as anyone other than Audrey Hepburn too," Miss Lansbury said. "And the funny thing is, I had read the book first! But that's the problem with film compared to books. When you read, you fill in all the blank spaces yourself, using your own imagination. When you see a movie, someone else has chosen what you will see."

"And if the actors are really great, like Audrey Hepburn, they 'own' the part," Robbie-Lee said.

"Well, she was great in the movie," Jackie said, "but I think I like the book better." She was still grumpy.

"I told you we should have read true crime or a mystery," Mrs. Bailey White said crossly. "Why can't we read a book about a person who's gone missing?"

God must have a sense of humor, 'cause at that very moment, the library's lights went out. We'd been half expecting an electric storm all day. Now here it was, in all its glory. You had to respect these storms. They didn't so much as arrive, they pounced.

I didn't mind thunder, especially the rumbling kind. Mama had convinced me, as a child, that thunder was "just some angels bowling in heaven." That took the sting out of my fear. But nothing Mama said could ever calm me when it came to lightning. A mean boy in school had told me that lightning was flames shooting from a dragon's mouth, and the image stuck in my head forever.

The library, I realized, was not a bad place to be in a storm. Miss Lansbury knew the layout like the palm of her own hand and, in no time at all, found a candle and matchbook she had put aside for emergencies. (Was there anything, I wondered, that a librarian *didn't* think of?)

The candle gave off very little light, just enough to create shadows whenever one of us moved even slightly. The window drapes were thin, and with each bolt of lightning, the room lit up like a set of flares on a pitch-black highway.

"Should we have a séance?" Jackie asked. I hoped she was teasing.

"I can lead a séance," Mrs. Bailey White piped up.

"Oh, please don't," said Priscilla, with more urgency than we were accustomed to from her. "It's not nice."

Jackie came to her rescue. "Of course we won't," she said soothingly. "We wouldn't do anything that upset you."

"We could pretend we're at summer camp and tell ghost stories," Robbie-Lee suggested.

"That hardly seems an improvement over a séance," Plain Jane said.

"I think we should do neither," Miss Lansbury said in her librarian voice. "I don't think the trustees of the library would like it."

"By the way," Jackie said to Miss Lansbury, "I've been meaning to ask you: what do the trustees think of us — I mean, our salon?"

"Well, our group has raised an eyebrow or two," Miss Lansbury said.

"What do you mean?" Jackie wanted details.

"Our board of trustees met last Tuesday and asked me to be there to answer some questions about our reading group." Miss Lansbury looked uncomfortable.

"What kind of questions?" Jackie's tone put us all on edge.

"They asked for the titles of the books we've been reading."

"They can't do that!" Jackie cried. "They have no right to get involved. It's government intrusion into our private business."

"Well, yes and no. They would have no right to look at your individual library cards to see what books you've been checking out. That's true. But as a group, we do meet at the library. We are a library reading group."

"What if we compromised?" I said, hoping to keep Jackie from blowing a gasket. "We don't give them the list, but we post it somewhere in the library for everyone to see."

"That's still giving them too much control," Jackie complained. "Next thing you know, they'll be trying to tell us what we can read and what we can't."

"Like they do in Communist countries," Robbie-Lee said.

"What else did the trustees say about us?"

Plain Jane asked. "Why are they trying to get involved at this point?"

"They said they have had complaints," Miss Lansbury said flatly. "I've had a few, myself."

Jackie harrumphed. "Is it the books, or is it us?"

"Let's not get sidetracked here," Miss Lansbury said firmly. "There is no need to get upset or take this personally. Frankly, I have the situation under control. I convinced the trustees that encouraging and providing a haven for a reading group is part of the library's mission. I told them that while they probably *could* ask to review our book list, that sort of oversight was heavy-handed and, well, un-American. The only thing they said was no pornography, no books on Lincoln, and no books that encourage deviant behavior or glorify violence."

"My goodness," Priscilla said.

"No violence — does that mean we can't read any books about true crime or about people who've gone missing? And maybe how to find them?" This was, of course, Mrs. Bailey White again. We all stared at her, considering what, if anything, to say. She looked even smaller in the candlelight, her pocketbook held tightly on her lap.

Robbie-Lee finally broached the taboo subject. "Mrs. Bailey White," he said gently, "what is this about 'finding someone'? What are you talking about? You are making us nervous by bringing it up all the time."

"Oh," she said. "I'm sorry." But she offered no explanation.

"Mrs. Bailey White has been through a lot, haven't you, dear?" Jackie said, reaching over to pat her on the shoulder, which seemed an act of great courage under the circumstances.

The storm, thankfully, was passing. We could hear the wind dying down, and the rain had slowed from pounding the roof like artillery fire to a soft, drizzly murmur that could lull a watchdog to sleep. We waited another fifteen minutes or so, long enough for the roads, which were surely flooded, to drain into the swamp. Mrs. Bailey White's intensity seemed to fade with the storm, and everyone relaxed.

Somewhere during the ride home, the conversation turned to Miss Dreamsville. Jackie, of course, is not the one who brought it up. We had turned on the radio to listen for static, just so we could keep track of the storm — the more static, the more danger from lightning.

Later I realized it must have been excruciating for Jackie to hear us chatting about Miss Dreamsville. Not one of us had figured it out, and like the rest of Naples, we were mystified.

"She's great," Robbie-Lee said. "I bet she looks just like Princess Grace or Audrey Hepburn. I wish she talked *more.* But I tell you what, she picks some darned good music."

Everyone agreed. Jackie simply nodded her head and kept driving. The night before, Miss Dreamsville's show had included "Unforgettable" sung by Nat King Cole; "I Left My Heart in San Francisco," Tony Bennett's new hit; "At Last" by Etta James; and two versions of Irving Berlin's "I'll Be Loving You, Always" — the one sung by Josephine Baker in 1926 (which, Miss Dreamsville explained in her breathy voice, was the first recording), followed by Frank Sinatra's version, recorded in '42.

This was much better than the usual sappy stuff we heard on WNOG, which led to speculation that Miss Dreamsville could not possibly be from Naples. Either that or the station manager — that guy from Canada — was picking the music. Looking back, maybe we should have realized it was Jackie, but like everyone else, we were blinded by the false picture of Miss Dreamsville we had created in our minds.

How Jackie managed to keep her mouth shut that night in the car is beyond me. Well, it turned out she did spill the beans, but only to Plain Jane after the rest of us had been dropped off. Maybe Jackie figured her secret would be safe with Plain Jane. After all, Jackie knew all about Plain Jane's masquerade as a sexy, in-the-know writer for the big New York magazines.

Plain Jane thought at first that Jackie was joking, and Jackie, she recalled, had been more than a little offended. "Well, why not?" Jackie asked. "Why couldn't I be Miss Dreamsville? Because I'm a housewife? With three kids?"

"Well, you were awfully surprised when you found out I was writing sexy stories for magazines," Plain Jane said.

Jackie had to admit that was true.

They continued their fussin' at Plain Jane's house over margaritas. Finally, worn out, they agreed to a truce. They would keep each other's secret. Plain Jane would choose when to reveal to their friends that she was in fact Jocelyn Winston, trendsetting writer on racy topics for important magazines.

But for Jackie, it was clear that the decision might be taken out of her hands — and not by Plain Jane. Friends can keep a secret but the world cannot abide a mystery for too long. The true identity of Miss Dreamsville was going to be revealed. When and how were the only questions.

EIGHT

There's an old southern saying that if you're worried about your weight, your clothes, or getting old, then you don't have any real problems.

I suppose there are two worlds — the small, protected one we carve out for ourselves, where we fret about a whole lot of nothing, and the other world, the real one, which comes knocking at the door, demanding to be let in and given a seat.

In Collier County, those real-world intrusions were so rare, no one could remember any. Change that was in the air nationally and even in our region — like the civil rights movement — always seemed to get to us last. Between the rednecks and the folks who visited from up north, that's the way most folks here wanted it, though sometimes I wondered if it meant we were going through life half-asleep.

Then, all of a sudden, we weren't far

removed from the one place in the world — Cuba — that every human being on the planet was focused on. For ten days that fall, we weren't a sleepy little backwater. Like everyone else in South Florida, we were right in the crosshairs of what was later called the Cuban missile crisis.

The Women's Literary Society did not meet. Lawns weren't mowed. Customers at the post office all but vanished. Our daily lives, even the fascination with Miss Dreamsville, were sucked into an empty space and replaced with fear.

We shouldn't have been so surprised. We'd lived through the Bay of Pigs fiasco the year before, when the US invaded Cuba, but it was a halfhearted effort and we knew the situation wasn't really resolved. All we had to do was turn on the radio to be reminded. The music from Havana radio stations had been replaced with *Radio Rebelde, Radio de la Revolución.* You didn't need to know much Spanish to figure that out.

But now we were told the Russians had been building nuclear missile sites in Cuba.

The whole idea of Armageddon coming in the form of a missile was especially unnerving. Previously, at Hiroshima and Nagasaki, atomic bombs had been dropped from the sky, which meant there was a plane involved. This required a setup that not every country could pull off. And it meant the intended target had a chance to prevent disaster — by shooting down the aircraft. But a missile was something else entirely. A missile could be launched from anywhere at any time.

After the Bay of Pigs, we didn't have much information to go on. Of course we were worried, but there wasn't anything we could do. But we began to get inklings there was fresh trouble brewing when the newspapers reported a huge increase of naval activity in Miami. This was confirmed by Ted, who had been there on a business trip. Next thing we knew, there was an announcement that President Kennedy was going to speak to the nation on the radio and television. The only TV station we could get was from Miami, and the reception wasn't too good, but you didn't need a clear image of the president to understand the seriousness of the situation. The Cubans, he said, now had nuclear missiles pointed at the US. It was no longer a question of them trying to build missile sites. They were already in place.

The president had a map that showed the likely range of the missiles. There were concentric circles starting in Cuba that ended as far north as Washington, DC. This

96

wasn't too clear on my television set, but I didn't need a map to realize that if you lived in South Florida, you were a sitting duck.

I was at home watching alone. I thought about calling Marty. I even considered calling Darryl. I knew that Jackie and Ted and their kids would be watching together from their living room sofa. Maybe Plain Jane would've joined them. Robbie-Lee and Miss Lansbury would be at their respective homes listening on the radio. But Mrs. Bailey White and Priscilla didn't have a television or a radio in their homes. Priscilla didn't even have electricity. Most likely, they wouldn't know until the next day.

Jackie said the twins were quiet — for once. They actually listened while the president spoke. When the announcement was over, Ted stood up and flipped off the set and said, "This is really serious."

Jackie had to fight the urge to get everyone into the car and start driving north, as far away from those concentric circles as they could get. But what she thought and what she said were two different things.

"We're going to act completely normal and do everything we usually do," she told her kids.

"Why?" asked Judd.

"Because we are not the type of people

97

who panic in the face of adversity." This from Ted, who was, after all, a World War Two veteran. This line of thinking had worked well for his generation.

"Oh," said Judd, not entirely convinced.

But this is the way the crisis was addressed, not just in the Hart household, as Jackie described it to me, but throughout Collier County and, for all I know, the entire southern part of the country. Since panicking was un-American, we suffered in silence, like a bunch of Christians facing the lions. Only one family in town was known to have built a bomb shelter, but they had been ridiculed as paranoid, so they had abandoned it. The rumor was that the shelter had filled with water.

The schools, churches, and stores stayed open, but activity was cut by half or more. Or maybe that's just the way it seemed to me. We spoke in funeral parlor voices, if we spoke at all.

Sorting the mail at the post office seemed ridiculous but comforting at the same time. I tried to stay busy. I just hoped that if a missile headed for Collier County, I'd be hit head-on. I didn't want to be around afterward.

We knew there would be no warning. Everyone understood that you might not be with your family when it happened. People made excuses to spend more time at home. I noticed more of the men who worked downtown were going home for lunch.

The Korean War vets were the only ones whose talk was full of bravado. I don't know why. They spoke about the possibility of an invasion by the Cubans and Russians. They were still thinking of old-fashioned warfare. "We'll meet 'em and fight 'em in the woods," they said.

The mayor came into the post office to study the maps that Marty had hung on the wall for tracking hurricanes. One showed the state of Florida. Another, the Gulf of Mexico and the states around it. And a third, labeled "Islands of the Caribbean," included the Florida Keys — and Cuba. We all knew that Cuba was ninety miles from Key West, and we weren't a heck of a lot farther north than that. When the Civil Air Patrol went looking for fishing vessels missing along our stretch of the Gulf, they could see the Cuban coastline.

I was beginning to think that a missile strike was inevitable when suddenly it was over. That's when everyone started acting crazy. People drank too much and got into fights. They drove too fast and got into accidents. Myself, I walked for hours along

99

the beach, not caring what I stepped on —
a dead fish, seaweed, shells. I didn't care. I
had an urge to run into the water, sharks be
damned, and start swimming straight out
into the middle of the Gulf. Maybe swim all
the way to Brownsville, Texas. I got home
just in time to hear Miss Dreamsville close
her show with Frank Sinatra's rendition of
"America the Beautiful."

Not that we could relax completely. Within
days, there were rumors about the CIA setting up shop deep in the swamps right here
in Collier County. A man named Curly
Brown said he came across a brand-new
building going up, a low-rise cement structure with no windows and a helicopter land-
ing pad on the roof.

Then another peculiar building popped
up, this one visible if you were out on the
Gulf, though oddly enough, it was said you
couldn't see the structure from the air.
Jackie's son, Judd, had seen it. Armed with
the confidence of his new name, Judd had
finally made a few friends and was out in a
motorized rowboat one day, fishing, when
they spotted it. Being twelve-year-old boys,
they had more curiosity than common
sense, and headed over to take a look. It
was a fortress, they said, a thick seawall with

a barbed-wire fence that crackled with electricity.

In the middle of all this tension, something almost funny happened. Maybe he got the idea from watching spy movies on rainy Saturday afternoons, but Judd Hart came up with a spectacularly bad idea. Someone, he thought, ought to learn Russian, the language of the Commies. After all, if the bad guys invaded, someone needed to know what they were saying. How else could we outsmart them?

So Judd decided to order some records from the Berlitz mail-order company. That was the difference between Judd and other people: maybe a few had the same thought, but Judd actually pursued it, and once he got an idea in his head, there was no stopping him.

The result of Judd's new hobby was like a bullet fired straight into a gas can at a bonfire. Judd's mistake was letting his fishing buddies in on his plan to learn Russian. They were the same two boys that had been with him when they saw the CIA building going up on the Gulf, and they begged Judd to teach them a few phrases.

Probably no one would have known what they were up to, except one day, not long after the Cuban missile crisis, they practiced

Russian over their walkie-talkies. Unfortunately, it was a Saturday afternoon and close enough to the VFW Hall that someone heard it on a CB radio. Since the veterans were drinking liberal amounts of beer and moonshine, it didn't take much for them to fly into a full-fledged mobilization. They couldn't speak or understand a lick of Russian, but by golly, the veterans knew Russian when they heard it. They leaped into their jeeps and headed into the swamps, looking for those damn Commies.

Later that day, Jackie was called down to the sheriff's department. When she arrived, she found Judd locked up in the whites-only cell, alone. Judd had persuaded the sheriff that he was the ringleader and to let the other two boys go home.

Jackie begged the sheriff, who was not the sharpest stick in the pile, to listen — really, truly listen — to what Judd had to say.

But the sheriff scoffed. "The boy is part of a Communist conspiracy," he said to the astonished Jackie, who couldn't wait to tell us about it at the next meeting of our reading group. Ted, arriving separately from Jackie, walked into the jail just in time to hear the sheriff say that Judd was "a tool" of the Commies.

"He's a *what?*" Ted yelled.

The sheriff ignored him. "Say something in Russian," the sheriff said to Judd.

"Zdravstvuite tovarishch. Gde ulitsa Gorkogo?" Judd replied.

"What the hell does that mean?" the sheriff demanded.

"Hello, citizen," Judd said calmly. "Where is Gorky Street?"

"This is absurd," Ted shouted. "The boy is just very intellectually curious. Can we please go home now?"

The answer was no. Ted asked to make a call and was directed to a pay phone in the hallway. He wanted his boss to hear this story from him, not anyone else. He told Mr. Toomb everything — about the Berlitz records, Judd's talent for language, the real reason the boy wanted to learn Russian.

To the surprise of everyone, Mr. Toomb had his driver bring him directly to the sheriff's department. Leaning on his cane, one of the most powerful men in the state hobbled into the building and went straight to the lockup. Judd, trying to be brave, stood up and came toward the iron bars.

"Young man," Mr. Toomb said, "I want to shake your hand. You are a true patriot."

Turning to the sheriff, Mr. Toomb added, "And you, sir, are an *idiot!*"

With that, they all went home.

NINE

In no time flat, the citizens of our small town got back to our normal, nitpicking ways. The men as well as the women. I guess we were all relieved to think about something other than atomic missiles.

Several of our town's most dedicated gossips had taken notice that Miss Dreamsville had chosen the 1945 version of Sinatra's patriotic song to celebrate the end of the crisis. Most people cried like babies and promptly forgot about the song, but a few suspicious minds began to wonder if this might be a clue to Miss Dreamsville's identity. But the would-be Sherlock Holmeses of Collier County didn't stop to think that Miss Dreamsville might actually be a member of the Sinatra generation. Instead, the rumors tended toward "Her father must have been in the war." We all missed a good clue, right under our noses, and Miss Dreamsville remained incognito, her most determined fans now fixated on making a census of every World War Two veteran in town who had a beautiful, young daughter.

Not everyone was enthusiastic about Miss Dreamsville. In the checkout line at the Winn-Dixie, I overheard one lady complaining that her husband now ignored her at night so that he could listen to "that Miss Dreamsville woman."

Another time, when I ran into Dolly O'Brien, the school nurse who had been friends with my mama years ago, she told me her job had gotten much harder on account of all the sleepy children (especially boys) who were staying up at night listening to "that woman" on the radio.

"It took me a while to figure it out," Dolly said. "I thought they all had influenza, or maybe mononucleosis, and then I realized they were tired. Just tired! The children in this town are not getting enough sleep!"

And, sure as the sun rises in the east and sets in the west, the various ministers in town decided it was necessary to speak out. Like most southern towns, we had a healthy abundance of churches — five Protestant and one tiny Catholic parish for the whites, and two colored churches. The number of Christian churches was surpassed only by the number of bait-and-tackle shops.

"Remember the story of Eve and the apple," warned the Very Reverend Barclay W. Willoughby of the Everglades Church of Christ Everlasting, who had his own radio show on WNOG, very early on Sunday mornings. He tried to convince the good citizens of Collier County that Miss Dreamsville was evil, but the more he spoke against her, the more folks loved her. Miss Dreamsville, it seemed, was here to stay.

I was as curious as everyone else about her, but the negative comments made me wonder about my hometown and the people who lived here. Some people were clearly having fun and were caught up in the mystery, but I was baffled by those who got worked up in an angry lather. Maybe, I thought, they were the kind of folks who just didn't like change. Or maybe, with so little to do, we just had a bumper crop of busybodies.

As for the literary society, our most recent book, *Breakfast at Tiffany's,* had resulted in Jackie's and Robbie-Lee's fussing at each other, which now seemed awfully unimportant after living through the latest threat from Castro. We tossed around some ideas, all of which failed to ignite until Jackie accidentally said something that got us onto a new path. "Oh, let's read something different, by someone unknown," she begged. "There must be so many great books we never heard of."

We were all silent, mulling it over, when Priscilla spoke up in her soft voice. "Zora Neale Hurston," she said. *Their Eyes Were Watching God."*

"Who?" Jackie said. "What was that title?"

"Their Eyes Were Watching God," Priscilla repeated. "It was written, oh, about twenty-five years ago. In 1937, I think."

"And the author . . . ?" This was Jackie, leaning forward.

"Zora Neale Hurston," Priscilla said.

"I'm afraid I've never heard of her," Miss Lansbury said apologetically.

"I never heard of her either," added Plain Jane, who looked around the circle to see if anyone had. The rest of the group shook their heads or shrugged.

"You haven't heard about her because she was a Negro writer, a woman Negro writer," Priscilla said. She had a way of saying things that were a little jarring, in just the right way — calmly, as a statement of fact, with no emotion.

"Well, tell us about her, and about that book," Jackie said in the soothing, encouraging tone she seemed to reserve for Priscilla. Coming from someone else, this could have seemed patronizing, but Priscilla always seemed to draw strength from Jackie.

"Zora Neale Hurston was a writer from right here in Florida," Priscilla said with a smidgen of pride in her voice. "She wrote novels, plays, and short stories. And stories about real people too. She was a great writer but she was also an anthropologist. A Negro woman anthropologist."

"How do you know about her?" This from Plain Jane.

Now Priscilla looked a little self-conscious. "Well, my favorite teacher from high school studied under her — under Zora Neale Hurston — at Bethune-Cookman College," Priscilla said. "Miss Hurston started a dramatic arts program there."

"But what was the name of that book?" Jackie was persistent.

Their Eyes Were Watching God.

"Let's read it!" Jackie exclaimed, clapping her hands together. Our group seemed susceptible to enthusiasm, so everyone agreed.

"There may be one problem," Miss Lansbury said. "I'm not sure how many copies I can locate."

"If you contact Bethune-Cookman's library, I bet they will loan us a few," Priscilla said.

"Oh! Good idea!" Miss Lansbury responded, looking a tiny bit embarrassed.

"Bethune-Cookman — isn't that where you want to go to college?" Robbie-Lee asked Priscilla.

"Yes," she said. "I mean, I hope to. Someday. If . . ."

"Well, Priscilla, if you set your heart on going to college, I'm sure you will make it happen." This was Jackie again, and I cringed slightly. Jackie did not understand how high the cards were stacked against Priscilla. This was the kind of advice you might give to a young person who was white.

"Well, let's get our hands on that book and read it," said Plain Jane.

Mrs. Bailey White cleared her throat and, inwardly, my heart sank that she might say something rebby. But I had underestimated her. "I don't think I've ever read anything by a Negro woman author," she said, "and maybe it's about time I did."

We weren't exactly a well-loved group in town, but once word got out that *our* library had borrowed books from a *Negro* college library, the tension escalated, even seeping more deeply into our private lives — for Jackie, especially. After the episode with Judd and the Berlitz records, old Mr. Toomb began to take more notice of the Hart household. After he discovered that Jackie was spending time with persons widely believed to be of questionable character, the old curmudgeon prodded Ted for an explanation.

Jackie saw this coming and tried to stay calm. "Why should Mr. T care?" she asked, when Ted raised the topic.

"It doesn't look right, the wife of his key financial adviser, cavorting with such an . . . unusual crowd." Ted was picking his words carefully. He knew he was tiptoeing his way through a minefield on a moonless night.

Jackie was frosting a cake, and without pausing or even looking up, she replied to her husband of fifteen years. "Don't ask me to give up my friends, Ted."

"I knew you'd say that," Ted said.

"Then why did you ask?"

"I thought you might be reasonable."

Jackie put the final flourishes on the cake. "It's just the Women's Literary Society."

Ted stood silently. Finally, Jackie looked at him. "I know — why don't you tell Mr. T that I'm a spy for the CIA and I'm keeping track of the undesirables?"

"Very funny."

"All right, here's a better idea — more palatable. Tell him that as a good Christian woman, I have decided to help these poor souls, in the hope that I may lead them to see the error of their wicked ways."

"Sarcasm is not helpful, Jackie." To avoid the temptation of throwing the cake at him, Jackie sat down in the breakfast nook and pretended to busy herself with straightening her reading pile — books, magazines, mail, and to-do lists. On top was *Their Eyes Were Watching God,* which she was two-thirds of the way through reading. The worn copy had the faint smell of mildew, even from several feet away.

"That book smells bad," Ted said.

"Of course it smells bad," Jackie said. "It's old, and this is Florida. All of our copies came from a Negro college. They don't have the money to replace books. And their library — you can bet on it — doesn't have air conditioning."

"What does that have to do with anything?" Ted asked softly. "What does that have to do with what we were talking about?"

"Everything. It has everything to do with what we were talking about. It's about life. The world we live in. I can't sit here and read another copy of *Good Housekeeping,* for God's sake!"

"Well, that's fine, Jackie. You go ahead and

read your radical books and hang out with your new friends. But you need to remember — all I'm trying to do is provide for this family."

Ted left the room, and pretty soon, she heard him rummaging around in the storage closet near the carport. This meant only one thing — he was going to Fort Myers to play golf. He didn't even say good-bye.

Ten

"I love that a woman wrote this, and I love Janie Starks," Miss Lansbury said breathlessly. "I'm ashamed I wasn't familiar with Zora Neale Hurston's writing."

"I'm so glad you liked it," Priscilla said, beaming. I noticed her maid's uniform had a big stain near the collar. She saw me looking at it. "Oh, I was carrying a tray, and I tripped on the rug and splashed Mrs. B's afternoon coffee all over me. Mrs. B says I'm awfully clumsy sometimes!"

"Priscilla, how come you're so darned nice?" Jackie said. "I think if I worked for that mean lady, I'd put poison in her breakfast cereal. Really, I think I would!"

Priscilla looked horrified. "Oh, shush, you must never say something like that, even though you're joking!" Our eyes all drifted over to Mrs. Bailey White, who seemed to have no reaction.

"Let's talk about the book!" Robbie-Lee

almost shouted. "It's brilliant, absolutely brilliant, don't you think?"

"Yes," Jackie said, "and how about Janie finding true love in her forties? And with a man *in his twenties?*"

"You would like that part," Plain Jane teased Jackie. "Anyway, what I see here is incredible insight and lyrical writing."

We were all busy dancing around the race issue, waiting (hoping) for Priscilla to bring it up, but she didn't.

"Mrs. Bailey White, what do you think?" Miss Lansbury asked, a bit desperately.

"I think it's the real Florida," she said.

"The *real* Florida? As opposed to the fake one, in which we live?" Jackie asked playfully.

"No, I mean it's about real people — a great big piece of the population — that we don't usually read about. I mean black folk, of course."

Now we were getting somewhere. But Robbie-Lee got us sidetracked. "I thought it was very romantic," he said wistfully, a tone that was unusual for him. "I can see why she fell for that fella, Tea Cake."

"And he didn't leave Janie," I added. "But what kills me is the way all those people in the town were always looking down on her. They were so quick to judge her and think the worst when she came back home." It dawned on me that I could have been speaking about myself.

"Can we get back to what Mrs. Bailey White was saying?" asked Jackie. Opening her copy of the book, she flipped some pages quickly. "Here it is — let me read this aloud. It's the opening sentence of chapter nine, and I think this is what Mrs. Bailey White meant: 'Joe's funeral was the finest thing Orange County had ever seen with Negro eyes.' Am I right, Mrs. Bailey White? 'With Negro eyes'? The whole book is seen with Negro eyes! And that, I think, makes it very unusual." You could practically see Jackie's mind working.

"Oh, I get it!" said Robbie-Lee. "There aren't even any white characters in the book. It's about Negro life. And love. And other stuff. I sure did find that hurricane scary."

"Sounds a lot like the one back in 1928," Mrs. Bailey White said. "That was a humdinger."

"Yeah, reminded me of how I felt when Hurricane Donna came through here. Dang."

"Well, the one in 'twenty-eight killed about two thousand people in the 'Glades," Mrs. Bailey White said.

"You all are getting sidetracked," Miss Lansbury scolded gently. "I've been doing some research, and before I forget to tell you, the town that is featured in the novel — Eatonville — was founded in 1887 near Orlando. Eatonville was the first incorporated black township in the United States! Now, I think that is so impressive. And that is where Zora Neale Hurston grew up."

"Hm," Priscilla said thoughtfully, almost to herself. "I guess that's why she was able to see things the way she did. She was raised in a place where it wasn't a spectacle, being colored. Everybody was just themselves, that's all. And you were just you. You weren't *colored* you. Am I making sense to y'all?"

"Perfect sense." Miss Lansbury beamed. "I can see this book means a great deal to you."

Priscilla removed her maid's cap and smoothed her hair with both hands. It seemed a nervous gesture for such a normally unflappable young woman. Her voice was soft when she finally spoke again. "Yes, I love the book," she said. "But I've never recommended it to anyone who is . . . not . . . Negro. I think most white people wouldn't read a book written by a Negro woman. But I thought you all might . . . like it."

Jackie reached over and patted Priscilla's knee. "Indeed we did, and I think I can speak for everyone that we are grateful to you for suggesting it. For sharing it with us."

This was starting to make my white, southern skin crawl. We just didn't have conversations like this. Priscilla, talking about race. Jackie, gushing about how swell it all was. I wanted to run out of the room. I shot a desperate glance at Robbie-Lee. He may have been a homosexual, but he had a man's gift for telling a joke to put everyone at ease.

He took the hint. "What do y'all think about a man named Tea Cake, anyway? Can you beat that? I mean, I love a good southern nickname, but that's a name that would be hard to live with! I can't get over that."

It made us smile, but it wasn't as funny as Robbie-Lee intended. There was an undercurrent of loneliness in everything he said. I looked around the group and saw they sensed it too. It wasn't obvious until you got to know him, but the sadness was sometimes there.

That night, as Jackie drove us home, we were a little quieter than usual. Maybe we were just thinking to ourselves. Or maybe we were just tired. The last thing we needed, or saw coming, was trouble.

We were halfway to Priscilla's grandma's house when we saw it — a light in the distance where there shouldn't have been one. "Oh, it's probably the police," Jackie said. "Maybe there's been an accident. They'll probably just let us go by."

"I think we should turn around," said Robbie-Lee.

"Me too," said Priscilla.

But it was too late. Our headlights illuminated two police cars blocking the way. Two men in uniform stood scowling at us, pump-action shotguns at the ready. They were both wearing Florida Highway Patrol uniforms and I remember thinking, *This ain't a highway, it's a damned dirt road. What are they doing here?*

Jackie stopped the station wagon and rolled down the window. She stuck her head out, with that wild red hair flying in every direction, and called out, "What's the problem, gentlemen?" This was brave but also smart. She let them see that the driver was a woman.

Searchlights from both police vehicles made it seem like daytime inside Jackie's station wagon.

"Don't move a muscle, no matter what," Robbie-Lee said through clenched teeth.

The two men approached with great caution. They crouched down and peered at Jackie, then at each one of us, and finally back at Jackie.

"License and registration," one of them grunted.

"I have to go into my pocketbook to get it," Jackie said.

"Just hand us the purse," said one. Jackie slowly passed her handbag through the window.

"Who are you looking for, Officers?" Jackie said politely.

They ignored her. "Where you from, lady?" asked one, picking through her wallet. "You got Massachusetts license plates and registration. But you got a Florida driver's license?"

"My husband and children and I just moved here from Massachusetts," Jackie said. "My husband works for Mr. Toomb. I got my new license but I haven't gotten the new plates or registration yet. You know how busy you are when you're moving . . ."

They weren't listening to her. They had jumped visibly when the name Toomb left Jackie's lips.

"Who else is in this car?" They studied us

again, and I thought for sure they would ask for IDs from all of us. But they seemed impatient now, ready to let us move on.

Just then, a third police car pulled up. This one came from behind us, and next thing we knew, we heard the familiar, grating voice of our sheriff. He joined the other two peering at us.

"Aw, hell," he said, and spat on the ground. "I know who this is. This is Mrs. Hart. Her husband works for Mr. Toomb. What we have here is the Ladies' Literary Society of Collier County. They are headed home from the library — one Boston bitch, one ex-con who murdered her husband, a man whose mother poaches alligators, a divorcée who works at the post office, and a *colored* girl."

The only one he didn't recognize was Plain Jane, who promptly provided him with her name and address.

"Say," he said, taking another look at me. "Ain't you the Turtle Lady? The one who was fool enough to carry that snapper across the road? You're lucky you didn't lose a finger or two. Or get hit by a damned truck." For some reason he found this funny.

"May we go now, please?" Jackie asked. "I really need to drop everyone off and get home to make sure my children did their homework."

They left us without saying another word.

We dropped Priscilla off, then had to face the possibility we'd encounter the police again on our way back. But there was no sign of them, except for some deep ruts that might have been made by the patrol cars.

For this to happen on the very night we had discussed Zora Neale Hurston's novel, it was enough to break your heart.

ELEVEN

The year-end holidays were approaching, which meant no one wanted to read anything that made us think too much. We chose Charles Dickens's *A Christmas Carol,* even though the author was a man and we'd each read the book several times. We needed safe territory after our incident with the highway patrol and the sheriff, and our nervousness showed in our choice of reading material. The book was short and had its scary moments but we knew it ended well.

Unfortunately, the book sent Jackie into a sentimental tailspin. She was missing cold weather, and so were her kids. Judd, she reported, was complaining nonstop that Collier County didn't "look, feel, or smell" like Christmas. "He misses it all," Jackie said, sounding wistful herself. "He keeps asking me when we're going to get chestnuts, and how we're going to roast them since we don't have a fireplace. He said, 'Mom, even the Christmas trees don't look like Christmas trees.' I told him that's because they are local pine trees, but that just made him sadder. He even asked me why there weren't any Salvation Army bell ringers here. I don't know what I'm going to do with that boy."

I tried to help by offering to introduce Judd to a Collier County tradition. Like swallows returning to Capistrano on a certain day each year, Yankees who came down for the holidays had an irresistible urge to jump into the Gulf of Mexico on Christmas Day. Frankly, the water was too cold even for them, but they stayed in just long enough to have a buddy take their picture so they could brag about spending Christmas in sunny Florida to their folks back home. The locals found this charade so amusing that we hurried our Christmas dinners so we could get down to the beach to watch. I took Judd, who was eager to go along. For an hour or two, at least, he forgot all about chestnuts and hot cider and all that Yankee stuff.

We never did find out what, or who, the police were looking for that night when we were driving Priscilla home, but we had our suspicions. There had been rumors of white civil rights workers coming to Florida to help mobilize the Negro population to vote.

Maybe some redneck had notified the highway patrol of a certain station wagon with Massachusetts license plates — Jackie's car. This seemed like a good time to lay low.

There was plenty to talk about in town, however, 'cause Miss Dreamsville was becoming unglued. We could tell what kind of mood she was in, based on the music she chose. People in town were in the habit of commenting on Miss Dreamsville's musical selections. It was no different from chatting about the weather. She was just part of our lives now. People would come into the post office, and if I was stuck working the counter, the chitchat would go something like this:

"Miss Dreamsville surely was in a mood last night. Sentimental, I'd say. Dang, those are some nasty clouds coming up over the Gulf." Or, "That Miss Dreamsville must've had a fight with her boyfriend. Why else would she choose that Skeeter Davis song? Or a whole set of Patsy Cline? Hope it stays warm this winter so I don't have to fill the propane tank."

Then Miss Dreamsville, whoever she was, went a little too far. She started talking, in her breathy voice, about the folk music movement in Greenwich Village. For our listening enjoyment one night, she played an entire set of Peter, Paul, and Mary, followed by Pete Seeger and ending with the Weavers.

"Miss Dreamsville done lost her mind," was the prevailing sentiment the following day. "That's Commie music."

Someone must have complained to the station, 'cause after that, we didn't hear folk music for a full three weeks. But then we noticed it reappearing once in a while, sandwiched between some good old country "love 'em and leave 'em" tunes.

Then, just to shake things up even more, Miss Dreamsville announced she had in fact broadcast live one night the previous week, hinting that there might be a repeat performance. This made people nuts, realizing that Miss Dreamsville, in the flesh, had been at the radio station and had they known, they could have got dressed, raced down there, and seen who she was.

This was the same week I let Marty the turtle go. I gave him a special snack — part of a tuna sandwich — and he went on his way. Sometimes they come back; sometimes they don't. Marty didn't, and to tell you the God's honest truth, it about broke my heart. Somehow that turtle and Darryl were linked, 'cause that same day, Darryl showed up at the post office again. This time he presented me with flowers, putting me on the spot, which might have been his intention. My stupid boss, Marty, said, "Aw, isn't that nice? He's not so bad, is he, Dora? Can't you just forgive and forget?"

Standing your ground after a public display like that is very hard. I'm reminded of those men who get down on one knee in a restaurant — right in front of everybody — and make a big to-do about asking the girl to get married. How the heck can she say no under those circumstances? (In some cases, could that, maybe, be the point?)

Before I became a member of the literary society, I think I might have given in to the pressure — sometimes said aloud, sometimes not — to go back to Darryl. But I had changed. My new friends didn't make me feel ashamed of being divorced. They seemed to like me, just as I was.

I smiled, accepted the flowers, then called him later and told him he was wasting his time. In the back of my mind, I'd been hearing that little voice that said marriage vows are forever. But it seemed to me that God wants us to be happy, and I couldn't be happy with Darryl.

Meanwhile, Jackie's marriage was falling

apart too, or at least ripping at the seams a bit. She and Ted had a huge fuss over — of all things — her station wagon.

Plain Jane told us what happened. There was such a ruckus at the Hart household that she heard the whole argument from her patio. The rest we got from Jackie.

It seems Jackie was making a Jell-O salad, the kind with marshmallows in it, for the twins to take to a Valentine's party. She was folding the marshmallows into the red goop at just the right moment, so they wouldn't melt. She was even wearing her "Best Mom in the World" apron that Judd had bought her one Mother's Day.

She tried — she really did.

But then the girls started having a fight in the other room, the kind of hair-pulling fuss that would only happen between sisters. Judd went outside and started sweeping the cement near the pool, but he made sure he was right in front of the kitchen window so Jackie would see him. He was sulking, not just because the twins were arguing again, but because he had asked for a puppy for his birthday, coming up in April, and Jackie had said no.

And then Ted walked into the kitchen. Poor Ted. He was as dense as a Florida tomato after a winter drought. Like a lot of men, Ted wanted to talk when *he* wanted to talk.

"Jackie, I want to speak to you about a new car," he said, just as she was moving the Jell-O salad into the fridge to chill. She didn't answer right away.

"Car?" she finally said. She started cleaning off the counter with a damp sponge. If you didn't get spilled drops of warm Jell-O off the counter right away, there'd be a stain that was hard to get out. Everyone knew that. Except men, I guess.

"I'm trying to talk to you about something important. What are you doing that for?" Ted asked.

"This is important," Jackie said. "The countertop will be ruined if I don't get this stuff off."

"Oh," Ted said.

Jackie was pissed. "Look, if I let these drops of Jell-O ruin the counter, we would have to replace it," she said through gritted teeth. "I am trying not to be wasteful — wasteful with money."

"Well, I am trying to tell you something nice, and all you can do is be angry."

Jackie finished wiping the counter and sat down at the breakfast nook, where she lit a cigarette as elegantly as if she was in a nightclub. "Okay," she said, finally looking at Ted. "Something about the car."

"Yes, I want to buy you a new car. Trade in the station wagon for a new one."

"I don't really think I need a new car," Jackie said. "Why don't we save the money for something else, like a vacation? Maybe for just the two of us? We could go somewhere, get away . . ."

"So you don't want the car?"

"Well, I don't see the point. Unless I were to get something different. The kids are older now; I don't really need the station wagon. I've never really liked station wagons, anyway."

Ted commenced to saying the single stupidest thing that ever come out of his mouth. "Why do you need anything other than a station wagon?" he asked. "You're just a housewife."

This dislodged a volcanic reaction in Jackie. She stubbed out her cigarette, grinding it into mush. *"Just a housewife?"* She shrieked so loudly even the twins hushed for a moment in the other room. *"Just a housewife?"*

It's a wonder the damn roof didn't blow off the house. She was beyond angry. She was nasty mad.

Still wearing her apron and slippers, Jackie left the house, slamming the door so hard it

129

sounded like a gunshot. All she had was her pocketbook and her car keys.

Once she was behind the wheel of the station wagon, she revved the engine like a wild woman. As she backed out of the driveway, she slammed hard into the mailbox — and to this day folks in the neighborhood still argue about whether she did it on purpose or not. Then she threw the car into drive, sped across the lawn and into the street. Who knew that station wagon could move so fast? She sent a plume of dust and sand into the air all the way down Paradise Court and as far as Magnolia Place, five whole blocks away.

Now Ted had to decide whether to call the police. His wife had just lost her mind and was driving at high speed who knows where in her Chevy station wagon. But if he called the police, she might be arrested, which would be the end of his employment with the Toomb family. On the other hand, if he didn't call the police, she would be a danger to herself — and everyone else in Collier County — until her anger wore off. Which could be a while.

"Dad, maybe you should go after her." This was Judd, looking wide-eyed and worried.

The twins did not seem overly concerned.

"Well, did she at least finish making the Jell-O salad before she left?" one of them asked.

Ted decided to sit down and light his pipe, which is what he did when he couldn't make a decision. This was interpreted by Judd as total disregard for what was happening with his mother.

Ten minutes, then twenty, went by. There was no sign of Jackie. Ted drove the twins to the party in his sedan. At home, he and Judd waited. And waited.

What they didn't know was that Jackie drove straight to Seminole Chevrolet in Fort Myers with the intention of trading in the station wagon. She got up there in record time and was still shaking with rage when she pulled into the lot.

She knew she looked ridiculous. There was not much she could do about the housedress and slippers, but she paused to put lipstick on, using the rearview mirror, before getting out of the car. Lipstick, in Jackie's mind, could fix anything. Or almost anything.

It was a Saturday afternoon in February and chilly, though not cold. She walked around the lot with two salesmen. "No station wagons," she said. "I'm trading in for a sedan."

But all the cars they showed her seemed boring. "Wait — how about that one?" she asked, pointing to a convertible, silver or maybe metallic gray. It looked like a space-ship. "My God, that is gorgeous," she said, rushing over to it.

The car that caught her eye was a 1960 Buick LeSabre. Because it was two years old, she could afford it. After negotiating with the men, she realized she would need only a small loan — $250 — to make up the difference for the value of the station wagon.

They went into the office to fill out the paperwork when one of the men hit the third rail on an electric train track. "Ma'am," he asked, "do you mind if I ask you — does your husband know you're here?"

All the joy of finding the perfect car was gone. "Well, no, he doesn't. And I don't see how it matters."

"Do you have two hundred fifty dollars in cash?" asked the other salesman, doubtfully.

"No, I shall need a small loan in that amount," Jackie replied, businesslike.

"We can't do a loan without your husband signing it," the first salesman said. "That's the way it is."

Jackie sat stiffly in her chair. "Well, gentlemen, I think that is patently ridiculous. And you have just lost yourself a customer." She left the showroom, walking slowly back to the dreaded station wagon. She waited until she'd driven a half mile before pulling over to the side of the road, where she cried. Now what? She could not go home. No, that would be a retreat.

She drove on. To Tampa.

She had been to Tampa only once but remembered vaguely that shady-looking used-car dealers had been in abundant supply. By the time she reached the outskirts of Tampa, she was too tired to be angry anymore. She just wanted to make a deal.

She drove from lot to lot along a seedy strip of used-car dealers on Dale Mabry Boulevard. By the fifth or sixth lot, she no longer bothered to park and get out of the car. She just pulled up within shouting distance of anyone who seemed to be working there and hollered out the window. She was determined to get the same make and model she'd so coveted in Fort Myers.

She didn't even know why she wanted *that* car, but she did. Later, she said it was like seeing the perfect prom dress or wedding dress, being ready to buy, and then being told you were too fat for it. Although darkness was now falling and she was tired, she was never more determined in her life.

Her hopes were raised at Sam's Super-duper Deals. They had the right make and model, but it was pink. Anyone worth their salt knows that redheads have trouble with pink. It has to be the right pink. Sadly, the car was what Jackie called Pepto-Bismol pink. "If it had been lipstick pink — you know, fuchsia — that would have worked for me," she explained later. "Or a very quiet, muted pink — delicate."

The salesman saw her disappointment. "Look, lady, my brother-in-law in North Tampa sells cars. I'll call him and see what he's got."

The news was good. A half hour later, at Billy Ray's Fabulous Steals and Deals, Jackie found the car she was born to drive. She'd been right about Tampa — there were no questions asked. She signed some papers and off she went. She was headed home, not sure what she'd proved, but feeling at the top of her game.

TWELVE

The car was the color of an overripe banana. No question about it, this was a car that belonged in Florida. Pale yellow bordering on cream-colored, the Buick was the same shade as the piña coladas that were served with a tiny umbrella at the Tiki restaurant on Highway 41 down near Miami. Robbie-Lee quickly dubbed the new car "the banana boat."

We kept telling Jackie that February was too cold to be driving a convertible with the top down, but that didn't stop her. She played the part to the hilt. In her white trench coat (from a place called Filene's in Boston), black driving gloves, and a cashmere scarf that she draped around her head and neck, she looked like a starlet. Plain Jane was the only one of us who seemed cool to the idea. "A convertible?" she said disapprovingly. "Two-door, no less? It's so impractical!"

"But that's what's so great about it," Jackie replied.

We didn't know, though, that the car was causing her a heap of trouble. The twins refused to be seen with her. They started taking the bus to and from school. If they missed the bus, they would walk. Judd had a different reaction: he and his friends thought the car was great, though they were disappointed she hadn't been able to get the one that was the color of a spaceship. They spent hours making the convertible top go up and down — just by mashing a single button on the dash — until Jackie made them stop. As for Ted, he was resigned to it.

But the real problem — little did we know — was that the Buick was making it harder for Jackie to come and go at the radio station. When you drive a car like that, you ain't gonna stay under wraps for long, especially in a town like ours, where minding other people's business is a time-honored tradition.

Jackie quickly learned to adapt and came to enjoy her secret even more, or so we learned later. To her, this was a whole new game. She would park the Buick behind the Baptist church or the jail, then walk to the newspaper office, where she still edited copy when they needed her, and to the radio station next door. On foot, no one noticed her, especially if she switched to flat shoes and the Miss Marple hat she'd picked up at the five-and-dime.

The most frustrated people in town were the teenage boys, who were getting more impatient by the week. At the soda fountain at the Rexall — where they hung out after school — or at the Dairy Queen at night, the conversation always seemed to loop back to Miss Dreamsville. Someone would come up with a new theory about her identity, based on a passing comment she'd made on her show, and an argument — Lord help us, even a fight — would break out.

Finally, three of the young, hormonally addled males decided to stake out the radio station. For several days, at all hours, we'd see them there, waiting. They reminded me of a lovesick dog that used to sit outside in the rain when Darryl's dog, Mazie, was in heat.

When they did not catch Miss Dreamsville arriving or leaving, the boys got fed up and stormed into the station, walking right past the "Silence Please" sign until they found the only person in the building — Mrs. Jackie Hart. Seeing her rummaging through a storage area, they assumed she was cleaning up (isn't that what women do?) and demanded, *"Tell us where she is!"*

"Who?" Jackie asked.

"Miss Dreamsville!"

"Oh, she left an hour ago," Jackie said, completely casual. She laughed after they left.

But in a way this wasn't funny. Not funny at all.

Without giving a hint that she was Miss Dreamsville, Jackie, at our next meeting, ranted about life and how unfair it could be. She felt "locked into" her role as housewife and mother. Sometimes, she said, it was necessary to shake things up, to rebel.

We thought she was talking about her new car.

When Jackie was in one of her moods, we were never sure what to say. Miss Lansbury, thankfully, spoke up. "I have a suggestion of something we could read next," she said in a tone that seemed meant to soothe Jackie's nerves. "There's a new book that was serialized in *Mademoiselle* magazine that I think we would like. It's called *The Feminine Mystique,* and it was written by a writer in New York named Betty Friedan." No one felt like arguing, so we agreed without any discussion.

That night, when Jackie drove us all home, we begged her to put the top up on the Buick; our southern blood was just too thin to have cold, damp night air blowing through our hair. With the top up, the Buick looked subdued, like a lady with a beehive hairdo squashed under a rain bonnet.

Still, the Buick was a beautiful car and a lot more interesting than the station wagon. As Robbie-Lee pointed out, we weren't likely to be mistaken for northern "agitators" while driving a sassy convertible painted a tropical color.

This was the night we met Dolores, Robbie-Lee's mother. We'd all been trying to get a gander at her each time we dropped him off, but she'd never come outside and we were blinded by the floodlights. But on this night, Robbie-Lee told us we were welcome to come inside. He sprang this on us, maybe so we wouldn't have time to think of any good excuses.

Robbie-Lee jogged to the front door and waved us in. I was glad we had dropped off Priscilla earlier; this would have been an awkward moment for her. She might have felt she should stay in the car rather than go inside a white person's home. Jackie, Plain Jane, and I edged our way slowly toward the house. We couldn't see a darn thing on account of the lights, and while it was true we wanted to see what Robbie-Lee's mother looked like, we got a bit more than we bargained for.

The house was, thankfully, not as brightly lit on the inside. In fact, a few minutes passed while our eyes got used to the change. We stood like a gaggle of gawky teenage girls, not sure what to do.

"Dolores!" Robbie-Lee called out. "We're here. Come on and say hello to my friends."

A once-beautiful woman slouched into the room wearing a pink bathrobe that had seen better days, just as the wearer surely had. The belt of the robe was tied high above her waist with the effect — intended or not — of creating a sling of sorts for her very large breasts. In the woman's left hand was a bottle of gin. In her right was a shot glass. A small cigar in her mouth finished the picture. "Howdy," I think she said.

As Mama used to say, no one on earth goes from cute to catastrophe faster than a Florida stripper. By the time they hit forty, they look like five miles of bad road.

Robbie-Lee pointed at each of us, one at a time. "This is Jackie, Jane, and Dora," he said. Dolores nodded.

"We'd better get going!" Jackie said cheerfully. "Nice to have met you! See you later,

Robbie-Lee!"

It was a fast getaway. I had to admire that about Jackie. She was smooth.

In the car, even though we knew we shouldn't, we picked apart every second of the surprise encounter.

"I bet she was gorgeous," Jackie said.

"Did you see her hands? They looked like an old man who's been out in the sun his whole life." This from Plain Jane.

"Well, she hunts alligators for a living," I said, not exactly in Dolores's defense. "And skins them."

"Did you see her chest?" asked Jackie.

"How could we miss it?" Plain Jane replied.

"She has a lot of trouble with her bosom," I said. "Robbie-Lee said that when she was young, she had her, um, breasts injected with something — God knows what — to make them huge. And now they hurt so much, she told Robbie-Lee she wished she could have them, uh, removed. She needs an operation, but the doctors she's talked to just laugh at her."

"Whoa," said Jackie. "That is sad! Poor woman."

"Funny how Robbie-Lee has to call her Dolores," Plain Jane muttered. "Never heard of someone calling their mother by her first name."

"Oh, I don't know," Jackie said. "I think that's interesting. Like she's an actual person, with her own personality, and not just someone's mom."

"Okay, this is very catty," I said, knowing they would slap me down unless I warned them that I was about to step over a line. "But do y'all think she was married when she had Robbie-Lee?"

"Oh!" said Plain Jane. "Probably not! But we shouldn't be talking like this about our friend's mother."

"That's right," Jackie said. "We shouldn't. End of conversation. Let's change the subject."

At our next meeting, Jackie told us she'd asked her kids if they would call her Jackie instead of Mom.

Their response? No dice.

"Forget it, Mom," Judd told her. "I'd rather call you *Mama* than Jackie."

She never brought it up again.

THIRTEEN

This is not hard to picture: Jackie devoured her copy of *The Feminine Mystique.*

She sat in her favorite chair for hours, her bare feet propped up on the coffee table. She didn't bother to get dressed — just stayed in that chair wearing a muumuu, one of those awful, shapeless dresses you could buy at the five-and-dime that make you look like you're wearing a flour sack.

Judd asked her once — only once — if she was all right. After she snapped, "Hell, yeah!" he left her alone. The twins tried a few times to get her attention but failed. Even standing directly in front of their mother and rolling their eyes didn't get the usual rise out of her. She just kept reading, looking up only to light a cigarette, drink a little Scotch now and then, or eat a chocolate bonbon. She got up just long enough to stretch, go to the john, and get a new supply of vices. She didn't even empty the ashtray.

First I heard about this was when I ran into Plain Jane in the fresh produce aisle at Winn-Dixie. Ted, she reported, had come home from a business trip, and he and Jackie had a big blow-up. Something, she said, about catsup.

Now that sounded mighty peculiar, even for Jackie. But Plain Jane, who'd been sitting out on her patio, said Jackie had left her kitchen window open, and half the neighborhood could hear the word *catsup* shouted hither and yon from inside the Hart household.

At our next meeting, Jackie told us about her fight with Ted, only she called it an "altercation." She was so mesmerized by *The Feminine Mystique* that she didn't even look up when Ted carried his suitcase in from the car. She didn't offer to do his laundry. She didn't prepare his favorite meal, as she often did when he'd been away.

Finally, he decided to get his own dinner. The kids had helped themselves to peanut butter and jelly sandwiches, so he was on his own. He opened the refrigerator and found enough leftovers to pull together a sad little meal of a hot dog and baked beans. But he could not find the catsup. He could not eat a hot dog without catsup. He never had, and he never would.

And so he marched into the living room like Sherman's troops tearing into Georgia.

"Okay, Jackie," he said, "where is the catsup?"

Jackie said she barely paused in her reading. "What? Is that you, Ted? Did you say something?"

"I said, 'Where is the catsup?' I can't find it. Is it in the cupboard?"

"How should I know?"

"Well, since you bought it at the store, I thought perhaps you would know where you put it."

"Ted, you know what? You have a college degree in business administration. You were a lieutenant in the Army. I have all the confidence in the world that if you put some effort into it, you can locate the bottle of catsup. All by yourself."

"You can't stop reading that book long enough to help me?"

Get it yourself!" she hollered loud enough to wake the dead. Then, Jackie said, she returned to her reading. She was, she said, beyond focused. She was ravenous.

She was the only one of us who had finished the book. In fact, she seemed to have memorized it, like a preacher who knows the precise location of every passage in the Bible. We couldn't keep up and didn't even try.

"This book describes exactly how I feel," she announced. She opened her copy and read aloud: " 'In the second half of the twentieth century in America, woman's world was confined to her own body and beauty, the charming of man, the bearing of babies, and the physical care and serving of husband, children, and home.' "

She read another passage: " 'Where is the world of thought and ideas, the life of the mind and spirit?' "

Jackie slammed the book shut triumphantly. "This author is right on target! All these women going crazy! Restless! Bored! And made to feel bad, as if somehow these feelings are our fault. I'd like to see any man stay home with a bunch of ungrateful kids, cooking, cleaning, and sewing, and let's see how many of them would have a smile on their face by the end of the day. Not all women are cut out for this. 'The Problem That Has No Name' — that's what the author calls the discontent that some of us feel. But you know what? The problem *does* have a name! I can sum it up in three words: 'just a housewife'! If I hear one more person use that expression, I think I will die. And that goes for men and women saying it. Especially women describing themselves that way!"

Jackie was talking so fast and with such intensity that her voice had become raspy. She left the circle to get a sip from the watercooler that sat outside Miss Lansbury's office. For a moment, I thought she was walking out, as if our circle couldn't contain her feelings and she needed to walk them off. But she came back and sat down.

Robbie-Lee cleared his throat. "I think it must be very hard to be a woman," he said cautiously. "I see what Dolores has been through."

"And who is Dolores?" Miss Lansbury asked politely. Driving her own car to and from the library had left Miss Lansbury out of the loop. I realized how much the rest of us had bonded during those car rides with Jackie.

"Dolores is Robbie-Lee's mother," I said, hoping to nip that conversation in the bud. I wanted to hear more reaction to *The Feminine Mystique,* not necessarily from Jackie but the others. Myself, the topic seemed somewhat foreign, I guess 'cause I didn't have children of my own and was divorced. While I could understand how Jackie felt, I couldn't feel it as deeply.

The following week, Darryl showed up again. He was staying at his aunt Martha's cousin's house, which was actually a farming homestead near Immokalee. There was no chance of talking privately at the post office and I didn't want him to come to my house. Against my better judgment (or maybe just so I could get back to work), I told him I'd meet him later at the Shingle Shack, Naples's only attempt at nightlife. I would have preferred to meet him at the Dairy Queen, but in the early evening, the place would be full of teenagers.

So the Shingle Shack it was, although I generally avoided the place because of the smell of old cigarettes and spilled beer. Darryl was already there when I arrived. He tried to smile when he saw me.

"How is the turtle?" he asked, trying a new tactic.

"You mean the snapper? The one you wouldn't help me with? He was doing fine, so I let him go."

"How do you suppose he got injured like that?"

"Must've been nicked by a car, or maybe a boat propeller," I said, realizing, at that moment, that I missed Marty the turtle more than Darryl the man.

"I always liked the way you helped turtles," Darryl said. "You have a gift."

"Don't flatter me, Darryl."

148

"No, I didn't mean it like that. I just admire the way you care for animals, especially the ones no one else'll take care of."

"I never really intended to become the Turtle Lady, you know," I said wearily. "People bring them to me and I can't say no."

"Then how come you can say no to me?"

I looked at the man I'd known my whole life and married at nineteen and wondered who he was. "Because . . . you've changed, Darryl. Maybe we were too young when we married."

"Aw, bullshit," he said. "Listen, Dora, things are going well for me. You should come back and see. Lots of new houses going up. Shopping centers. All over the state. I can't get enough men to fill all the jobs. Soon it's gonna happen here too."

"What's going to happen?" I asked.

"Land development," Darryl said with a cocky grin. "You should see what they're planning for Orlando. The whole damn state is going to be paved over."

"I don't want the whole damn state to be paved over." All I could think of was, *Where would the turtles go? And the birds? Alligators?* I hoped Darryl was completely wrong. As for Orlando, I couldn't imagine hordes of people moving to a little sunbaked town like that. At least Naples was on the Gulf. "Why is all this a good thing, Darryl?"

"Because it's *money,* Dora." He looked at me as if I was simpleminded. "Naples will be developed too, mark my words."

"What makes you so sure?"

"Because there are some very smart people behind the scenes making sure the rich folks who move to Florida choose Naples," he said.

"And how will they do that?"

"Fishing and boating," Darryl said.

I laughed. "Just about every place in Florida has good fishing and boating," I said.

"But not every place has golf courses," Darryl said. "Not *first-rate* golf courses, like the ones being planned, right now, for Naples. And don't forget our location at the bend of the Tamiami Trail. When more folks come through here, they'll be needing places to stay before they drive through the Everglades to Miami. So there'll be a need for some big hotels."

I thought of Jackie, and the other Yankees, who talked about being scared to death to drive the part of the Tamiami Trail between Naples and Miami. At seventy-five miles per hour, you could be there in less than two hours, but you'd better not let your mind wander. That stretch was a pitch-black two-lane road with deep drainage ditches on either side. Even the locals knew you could end up as alligator chow if you made the smallest mistake. If more Yankees were headed to this part of Florida, I could imagine that they'd want to stop here and rest up for the nail-biting drive to Miami.

But I was bothered by Darryl's attitude. "You really *have* changed, Darryl," I said.

He had to stop himself from pounding his fist on the bar. "Damn it, Dora, I am trying to tell you that you should *come home.* We can get remarried; I'll forget you ever left. I'll forgive you."

"No, thanks, Darryl." I spoke so softly, I wasn't even sure I'd said it out loud. When I looked at his face, I knew I had.

"Well, good luck, Dora," he said. "I mean, good luck finding someone else who'll marry you. You'll never find anyone! You'll probably never have kids. I bet you'll never live in a really nice house. Are you still living in that crummy place that was in your father's family? Huh? Have you really thought about what you're giving up?"

That weekend I stayed entirely by myself, not venturing out. In the back of my mind I always thought I might, or could, go back to Darryl, like maybe I hadn't shut that door tightly behind me. Either that, or I'd look for somebody else. But now I kept thinking about Jackie and *The Feminine Mystique.*

I wondered how many women, right in Collier County, felt the same as Jackie and the women in the book. Surely some of them — maybe many of them — *were* as happy as they appeared to be. But I kept thinking of the women who came into the post office, usually with three or four children in tow, who looked so miserable, it scared me. It was pretty common for them to say something (when no man was around) that was clearly a complaint, maybe even a cry for help. They were the ones who had bought the dream — hook, line, and sinker — but maybe it hadn't been the right dream for them, and they couldn't understand why they weren't happy.

And then it hit me. Could it be that some of these women were envious of *me?* I felt a stab of guilty pleasure. Yes, I suppose so. Because I had one thing they didn't have — freedom.

At the next meeting, Mrs. Bailey White and Plain Jane said the book had confirmed what they'd been thinking for years. "You know, when I was young, I think women were more independent. Women had just gotten the right to vote," Mrs. Bailey White said. "Then it seemed like we started going backward in some ways."

"Yeah, think of all the women who worked during World War Two," Plain Jane said. "I worked for an insurance company in Tampa, and I loved it. I sold more policies than anyone. But when the war ended, they took my job and gave it back to the man who'd had it before he left for the Army."

"So all you gals want to *work?* This is about having jobs?" Robbie-Lee said. "I was always kind of secretly envious that women didn't have to work. Seemed pretty nice to stay home, make curtains, and all that. That's just not an option for men."

This was food for thought. "That's interesting, Robbie-Lee," Jackie said quietly. She looked tired. "The book is about women and our lack of choices, but as you say, men are limited in their choices too. Priscilla, what do you think?"

Priscilla had been completely silent. "Come on, Priscilla, we would love your opinion," Jackie said in her gentle tone.

Something was amiss. I couldn't put my finger on it. Jackie continued to encourage Priscilla, but this time her effort missed its mark. Priscilla looked down at her hands and picked at her nails.

"Maybe Priscilla doesn't feel like talking," Miss Lansbury said. Sometimes she had a gift for stating the obvious.

"No, no, actually I do have something to say. I'm just not sure how to say it."

In the long, empty moment that followed, a feeling washed over me that I couldn't quite place. Uneasiness, I suppose.

"Well," Priscilla began slowly, "I was surprised that so many women were unhappy. And I had to ask myself, *What have they got to be so unhappy about?* Most of us colored women would give anything to have the problems described in the book. I mean, Negro women have always had to work. We have to, because our men aren't paid a fair wage. Compared to white men, I mean. And obviously, there are some jobs — the *good* jobs — that colored men can't get at all, through no fault of their own. So the women — colored women — we have had to hold hearth and home together. One way or another, we need to bring money into the household. That could mean picking crops in the field, like my grandma, or working for a white family, like I do. Even the women who seem like they're not working — well, they're taking in laundry or ironing or mending. So I guess what I'm saying is that the problems these ladies are talking

154

about in the book — those are luxuries most colored women don't have."

Jackie sat back in her chair with a jerk.

Miss Lansbury, using a calm voice, tried to steer the conversation. "So what you are saying, Priscilla, is that the Friedan book may apply more to white women?"

"Yes," Priscilla said, her eyes downcast. "And I don't mean to be insulting to anyone's experience; that's just my, uh, point of view."

"And that's certainly a valid point of view," Plain Jane piped up, speaking rapidly. "One of the things I love about this group is that we can say what we think! And this is an example of someone opening our eyes! Myself, I am a little ashamed I didn't see that when I was reading the book."

I stole a glance at Jackie. She looked stunned. You could always tell when Jackie's mind was spinning. Her eyes seemed unfocused, as if she was trying to peer into a murky pond, determined to see the bottom.

On the way home, Jackie was noticeably quiet. I think we all assumed she was offended. With each minute that passed, Priscilla sank farther down in the seat beside me.

I don't know what possessed me, but I tried to rescue all of us — and especially

Priscilla — from Jackie's silence. "I would just like to say," I began, my voice squeaky, "that this was a very meaningful evening tonight. I think it was very brave and honest for Priscilla to tell us what she thought about *The Feminine Mystique*."

I instantly knew I'd just made things worse. I went on, hoping to correct my blunder. "And I think it's wonderful that we are all friends and that Priscilla is part of our group, and I hope we always stay friends, because I love our friendship, and besides, by being friends we are changing the world for the better, I think, one friend at a time."

I sounded like I'd just won the Miss Congeniality award at a third-rate beauty contest. I was hoping someone would pick up the thread — Robbie-Lee, for example, but he seemed in over his head on this topic.

No one knew how to follow my goofy, rambling speech. But one nice thing happened — Priscilla reached for my hand and squeezed it.

We learned later that Jackie was crushed by Priscilla's comments, not because she thought they were unfair or unkind but because they were dead-on right. This, unfortunately, made Jackie even more upset, because on top of everything else, she felt guilty.

Plain Jane and Jackie had a fight about it later that night, after they'd dropped the rest of us off. They didn't let on at the time, because if they had, they'd have revealed their secrets to the rest of us. Plain Jane admitted that she started it by demanding to know why Jackie had been so quiet when she — Jackie — was usually the one who encouraged Priscilla.

"I'm just confused, that's all," Jackie said. "I was afraid of saying the wrong thing, of making things worse. I'll think about it and deal with it later."

"That's cowardly!" Plain Jane almost screamed. "It's what you say at the moment that counts! Later is too late."

"Look — you're not married, and you don't have kids, so you don't have the same kind of pressure!"

"What has that got to do with anything?"

"The Friedan book doesn't speak to you the way it speaks to me," Jackie replied. "That damn book made me see a lot of things clearly! And then I realized what a fool I am — so caught up in myself — that I didn't realize how Priscilla would see it. And I feel like a total idiot! I just want to go home and have a drink."

157

And Jackie did something she almost never did in front of anyone. She cried.

Now of course that made Plain Jane feel terrible and they agreed to bury the hatchet. "Come in the house and I'll fix you a mimosa," Plain Jane said. "I don't think we should end the evening this way."

The discussion over mimosas and cocktail nuts was much calmer. "You know," Plain Jane said, her voice a little woozy after her second drink, "I think I am part of the problem. Those books and articles I write — sex on a desk and all that crap. I'm putting all kinds of stupid ideas in women's heads. I mean, women actually read that stuff. And believe it! Oh my God, what have I done?"

"Well, I wouldn't beat yourself up like that," said Jackie, by now two or three sheets to the wind herself. "I mean look at me — Miss Dreamsville! What kind of garbage is that!"

"But you're proving a point! Wait till everyone finds out. You can show everyone that a middle-aged mother can be beautiful and sexy. You'll be breaking down stereotypes!"

"Oh, I don't know." Jackie was sleepy or maybe just plain worn out. "What kind of role model am I? I mean, can you read

Vogue, love fashion, flirt with men, and still believe in female emancipation?" She lit a cigarette although there was already one burning in the ashtray. "Well, I don't see why not," she said, answering her own question. "Maybe freedom means defining yourself any way you want to be."

"Well, we are a long way from that happening," said Plain Jane. "At least here in Collier County, I don't see a whole lot of improvement anytime soon. I think we're sort of locked in place on this issue, Jackie."

This was an honest statement, but not one Jackie wanted to hear.

FOURTEEN

I got a frantic call from Jungle Larry's Safari, hoping I would help them with an ailing snake.

"But I don't do snakes," I reminded Larry, a nice-enough man who had retired, along with some weather-beaten animals, from a traveling circus. "Try the vet in Everglades City."

I didn't have anything against snakes but they were outside my area of expertise. And besides, I figured I'd never have the option of getting married again — assuming I'd want to — if I became known as the Snake Lady. Turtle Lady was bad enough.

The next meeting of our reading group was the following day. I hoped the evening would go more smoothly than the last time. I saw right away — and was relieved — that everyone seemed to feel the same way. *The Feminine Mystique* had caused enough trouble.

Miss Lansbury was even prepared for a diversion: she suggested we read aloud from *Little Women,* and we quickly got into it, passing the book around the circle. For some reason this was strangely soothing, like drinking tea with honey when you've got a nasty cold.

Of course every one of us, except Robbie-Lee, had read *Little Women* several times. The story was all new to Robbie-Lee, which was kind of interesting to watch, almost like reading the book again for the first time. He even cried when he realized sweet little Beth was going to die. This in turn made the rest of us cry, but it was a healthy kind of weeping — a tonic of sorts.

Miss Lansbury pointed out that critics sometimes pooh-poohed *Little Women* by calling the book a "domestic drama." Jackie harrumphed. "Of course it was a domestic drama, that's all women were allowed to do — stay home! The men go away to war, they go to college. I hated it — still do — when Laurence goes off to college, leaving poor Jo behind."

Jackie, it seemed, was still grappling with *The Feminine Mystique.*

"But what's fascinating — is it not? — is that a great deal actually goes on within the March household." This was Miss Lans-

161

bury. "It is the *relationships* that matter. It's an ingenious depiction of a sophisticated social sphere — the world of women."

This was loftier than we were in the mood for. "Oh, let's just keep reading the book," said Mrs. Bailey White. "Forget all that other stuff."

In the car on the way home, Plain Jane made an interesting point. "With all the times I read *Little Women* when I was growing up," she said, "would you believe I never really noticed — until tonight — that the father in the story isn't present because he's a chaplain in the *Union Army?* I just thought of him as having 'gone off to war.' It's a wonder they allowed us to read that book south of the Mason-Dixon line."

"Maybe that's because the father is a chaplain. He's not actually gone off to kill anyone. Maybe that made it all right." This from Jackie.

"And he's not a main character," Priscilla added. "I mean, as a character he is mostly absent."

"I think it's because the book is about a family and you become attached to them as *people,*" I suggested. "You don't think of them as Northerners, even though it's very clear they live up north. They could be anywhere. It could be set in the South, with

162

the father serving as a chaplain in the Confederate Army."

This left everyone thinking to themselves. "We should talk more about this at our next meeting." This from Mrs. Bailey White. But no sooner had she spoken than we noticed something odd — a strange smell in the night air like burning leaves. The odor got stronger and Jackie panicked, thinking the Buick's engine might've caught fire. She shut off the motor, right then and there, and asked Robbie-Lee to look under the hood.

"No engine fire," he reported a moment later, "but something is definitely burning ahead." He sounded anxious, which had the effect of unsettling the rest of us.

"Well, it can't be a swamp fire," Mrs. Bailey White said. "No way. Not with all this rain lately."

"Oh my God," Priscilla said, her voice trembling, "maybe one of the houses is on fire."

"Well then, let's go as fast as we can and see if we can help," Jackie said. Her voice was almost unrecognizable — about a whole octave higher than usual. She hit the gas before anyone could think of what to say.

The sky grew brighter as we continued. "I think we should turn around," Robbie-Lee said. "Or stop here and I'll go ahead on foot and see what I can do to help."

"There is nowhere to turn around, except at the church," Jackie replied. The church would be coming up on our left, just past the one sharp bend in the road. The houses were beyond it, perhaps a half mile. I remember asking Priscilla why the church wasn't built closer and she had smiled. "The church was built first," she explained. "This was right after slavery days. Once they decided to live here, they picked the best piece of land for the church. They cleared the land there and slept on the ground. It wasn't till later they built the houses, one by one."

Just as I was remembering these words, we rounded the bend, and Jackie hit the brakes so hard, I smacked my forehead on the seat in front of me.

Standing straight in front of us were five men in white robes, torches in their hands.

Had they been waiting for us? Or had they seen car headlights headed their way and planned to stop anyone who happened by? Then I saw the rest of them. There were another eight, maybe ten, in the clearing next to the church.

It was the church that was on fire. Even during the few seconds that had just gone by, we could see the blaze was growing worse. Flames burst through a section of the roof. An arc of fire leaped from the roof to an old-time revival tent set up beside the church, on the lawn. The tent didn't burn, it exploded, tearing itself loose from the ropes that had secured it to the ground.

The most peculiar thing was that the men in robes and hoods — the five that were standing dead ahead in the road — did not turn to look at the progress of the fire. The flames were wild as a hurricane and (to me, at least) surprisingly loud. And yet these men, these strange inhuman creatures, had no reaction, which made them seem even scarier, if that was possible.

Eight or nine seconds passed. I realized that Priscilla was whimpering or maybe praying. Someone else — Mrs. Bailey White — was saying, "Oh. Oh. Oh."

I heard my own voice saying, "Priscilla, get down." I pushed her to the floorboard and took off my coat, covering her with it. I knew this probably wouldn't fool anyone, but it was the best I could do. Mrs. Bailey White followed suit, unbuttoning her cloth coat and laying it on top of mine.

"Priscilla, lay as flat as you can," Mrs. Bailey White said.

Not a peep came from the front seat until

suddenly Robbie-Lee said, "Back up." Jackie made no attempt to put the car in reverse, and he repeated, "Back up. Back up! *Now!*"

Plain Jane started yelling, "Turn around, Jackie, turn around!"

But there was no way to turn around. The road was barely one car length wide.

"Don't turn around! Back up!" This was Robbie-Lee.

"Oh, shut up!" screamed Jackie. "Don't tell me what to do." And then she did something that shocked us all. She didn't back up. She didn't try to turn around.

She stomped on the accelerator.

The big Buick growled and the wheels dug into the soil, spewing sand and whipping the car from side to side until the tires took hold. We were all screaming, even Priscilla, I think, from underneath the coats. I got a glimpse at Jackie and knew we were all goners. Her eyes were bugging out in a way I didn't think possible. She was screaming loudest of all, gripping that wheel — and aiming right for the Klan guys like a kamikaze pilot. At first they didn't move, then scattered like yard birds when they realized the driver of the car wasn't fooling.

Jackie yanked the wheel to the left and headed for the other Klansmen. She clipped one man and hit a second one hard enough

166

that he bounced across the hood of the car. His watch — or something — hit the windshield, leaving a large scratch or mark. Jackie just kept going. We drove behind the church and came around the other side, past where the revival tent had stood until a few minutes earlier. Bouncing so hard in our seats that we couldn't speak, we assumed Jackie had gone completely mad, and there was nothing left to do but try to hang onto each other or a piece of the car interior. As we lurched back onto the road, now heading back to Naples, I heard a sound I'd been expecting — a shotgun blast — but it was aimed wildly and didn't come close.

Jackie continued to make a beeline toward Naples. After a while, though, she slowed down, finally coming to a stop.

"What the hell are you doing now?" said Robbie-Lee.

"You drive," she said in a faraway voice. "I can't . . ."

Robbie-Lee climbed over Plain Jane and Jackie and squeezed himself behind the wheel.

Priscilla had dug herself out from the coats and was gripping the seat back in front of us. "Where are we going?" she asked. "What are we going to do?"

"We have to go somewhere and think,"

Plain Jane said.

"My house," said Mrs. Bailey White. "No one goes there. You can pull the car around back."

This option was so obviously the right one that no one suggested anything else. Robbie-Lee drove fast — almost recklessly — and glanced in the rearview mirror every few seconds. But no one followed. *Not yet,* I thought.

When we reached Mrs. Bailey White's meandering driveway and made our way toward the house, I could almost breathe normally again. Mrs. Bailey White directed Robbie-Lee to drive toward two mimosa trees, which seemed to make no sense at all until we were up so close, we could see a narrow path — not much wider than the Buick — that would take us around back. When he turned the headlights off, the night sky was so dark, I thought it might swallow us whole.

All we had to do was follow Mrs. Bailey White about twenty feet to the back door. Robbie-Lee had to carry Priscilla. Then he went back for Jackie. I couldn't tell which one was in worse shape. We settled them into large, heavy chairs that faced each other by a fireplace. Robbie-Lee commenced to building a small fire, while Plain Jane and I tried to make Priscilla and Jackie comfortable. Once the fire got going, we realized that both of them were suffering from some sort of shock but were slowly coming around. Mrs. Bailey White pulled down the shades and closed the hurricane shutters.

"If anyone sees a little light from the fireplace or smells the smoke, don't worry, that will seem normal to them," she said.

"Nice firewood," Robbie-Lee said. "Where do you get it?"

"Chop it myself," Mrs. Bailey White said proudly.

"Don't you have electric in this house? What about heat?"

" 'Course I got electric, and I also got a furnace and an oil tank." Mrs. Bailey White seemed a little miffed. "I just like to do things the old-fashioned way."

Despite the gravity of our situation, Robbie-Lee could not resist studying the room with a professional eye. "Love the wallpaper. Is it vintage?"

"I guess you could say that." Mrs. Bailey White almost laughed.

"And those ceramic jars there on the mantel," he added. "That's quite a nice collection. Are they cookie jars? I notice they don't match exactly, but that's what makes them special."

"They're not cookie jars, they're urns," she said. "The one on the far left is Grandma. The one next to that is Aunt Fern. This one over here" — she pointed to a third one — "that's my late husband. And next to him are the dogs. I put them all together."

I give Robbie-Lee a lot of credit. His eyebrows reached toward heaven but otherwise he didn't move a single muscle. I'm sure I recoiled, but I was not, thankfully, in Mrs. Bailey White's line of vision. Even Jackie and Priscilla, who had barely been opening their eyes, turned to stare at the mantel. That's when I knew they were both going to be all right.

"You mean . . . they . . . these people . . . your family . . . were *cremated?*" Robbie-Lee had finally found his voice. Most of us were good Baptists or Methodists and expected to be buried six feet in the ground. I had never even heard of anyone in Collier County being cremated and, apparently, neither had Robbie-Lee.

He tried changing the subject. "So, how old is the house? Nice wainscoting, by the way."

"Could we stop the chitchat, please?" demanded Plain Jane, seated next to me on a leather sofa the size of a hippopotamus. "I think we have more important things to discuss. Mrs. Bailey White, please, come sit here so you can hear everything that is said." Mrs. Bailey White obeyed, and Plain Jane continued. "Could someone please explain to me what happened tonight? And what we are going to do now?"

No one answered, which seemed to irk Plain Jane even more. "Jackie," she demanded, "please explain." And then came the words as acidic as year-old cider vinegar: "You could have gotten us killed."

Jackie tried to answer. "I was trying to . . . get us out of there," she said finally.

"Why the hell didn't you back up or turn around?" Plain Jane was shouting now.

"Well, I *did* turn around."

"Okay, you two, stop your fussing." This from me. "Let's be grateful we are all here, alive. Especially . . ." I didn't have to say the name. I meant Priscilla, who would have been their prime target, though who knows what they would have done to the rest of us.

Robbie-Lee crouched by the fire, snapping a few small sticks in his hands and flinging them into the flames. Instead of looking at each other, the way we did in our circle at the library, we stared mindlessly at the humble fire. How odd, I thought, that we looked at this fire as a source of comfort. An hour or so before, a fire meant something else altogether.

"I don't know if this will be helpful," I heard myself saying, "but Mama used to say that when you don't know what to do, do nothing. She meant you can try too hard to solve a problem. If you give it a little time, the answer might just come to you, plain as day."

No one objected. I was hoping Plain Jane would calm down and Jackie and Priscilla would recover a bit more. We needed all of our brains working together to figure this one out. I assumed we probably had two choices, neither of 'em good. We could lie and deny we were ever there. Or we could go to the police — the sooner, the better — and tell them what happened, although this was risky since the Klan and the police were known to be friendly and rumored to be in cahoots with each other.

Priscilla had curled up in a little ball, her shoes kicked off and her feet tucked under her. In some ways, Jackie was in worse shape — limp and defeated.

But Plain Jane was not through with Jackie. "You know, I grew up in the South, and one thing you don't do is tangle with the Klan." She hurled the words in Jackie's direction.

Jackie didn't react at first, but then she surprised us. In a low, weary voice, she said to no one in particular, "I was in a bad fire once. A long time ago."

"Really?" asked Robbie-Lee, when she didn't say more. "What happened?"

Jackie sighed. "As I said, this was a long time ago." She paused, and then: "It was terrible. Completely terrible."

Now we had to know. "Where was this fire?" This from Priscilla in a tiny voice. Until now, she'd been silent.

Jackie looked at Priscilla, then at each of us, one by one. "During the war. At a nightclub. In Boston. I wasn't supposed to be there. My parents thought I was at a friend's house."

Just when we thought she might not say anything more, she added, "It was a famous fire. You may have heard of it. The Cocoanut Grove fire."

"Oh my God," said Plain Jane. "Yes, I heard of it."

"Me too," said Mrs. Bailey White. "I read about it."

The younger ones among us — Robbie-Lee, Priscilla, and me — were only vaguely aware of the story. When Jackie seemed unable to continue, Plain Jane said to us quietly, "Mostly young people were killed."

"Four hundred and ninety-two people, to be exact," Jackie said. "There were only supposed to be five hundred in the club, but there were about a thousand. The doors were locked from the outside so no one could sneak in without paying. To this day, I don't know how I got out. I think maybe someone carried me."

"But when we saw there was a fire tonight, up ahead of us, you drove toward it." This was Priscilla.

"Don't think I didn't want to run away," Jackie said, "but all I could think of was your grandma being trapped in her house."

Priscilla and Jackie locked eyes. "Thank you," Priscilla mouthed the words.

"So when you actually saw the fire — the church — is that why you reacted the way you did?" This was Mrs. Bailey White. "You panicked?"

"No," Jackie said. "Of course I was shocked when I saw the flames. I hadn't seen a building burn like that since . . ." Her voice trailed off. "But there was something else too. When I was a little girl, we were visiting my aunt and uncle on Long Island. And we ran into the Klan."

"On *Long Island?*" several of us cried out. Jackie waited for us to settle down before continuing. "Yes, on Long Island. I'm not sure where, someplace near the eastern end. My father was driving; my mother was sitting next to him. I was in the backseat, mostly asleep. And we came around a bend in the road — just like tonight — and there they were, these men. In their robes. Holding torches. They had blocked the road; there was nothing we could do. My father drove forward and had to face them."

"But they let you go, of course," Plain Jane said quickly. "You're white."

"Well, yes, but we had a very bad moment. They asked for our names and where we were from, and one of the men said to the other, as if it was a dirty word, *'Catholics.'* And he spat on the ground."

"You're a Catholic?" said Robbie-Lee, clearly surprised.

"I was raised a Catholic," Jackie replied. "But I became a Unitarian when I married Ted."

"What's a Unitarian?" asked Robbie-Lee.

"It's church, without God," Plain Jane said.

"Don't be silly," Jackie snapped, and almost laughed. "Unitarians are a type of Protestant. They're just a little less structured than, say, the Methodists or the Baptists."

"Excuse me — could we get back to the story on Long Island?" This was me, feeling impatient and being more rude than I had ever been in my life. But I wanted to understand.

"Yes, yes," said Jackie. "They taunted my father and mother because we were Catholics. I think they hoped we would deny it, but my father would never have done that, not in front of me, anyway. He said, 'Yes, we are Catholic.' And I remember wondering what would happen next, because clearly, to these men in their white robes and torches, being Catholic was not a good thing."

"What happened then?" Plain Jane asked the question the rest of us were afraid to ask.

"Another car came up behind us. This diverted their attention away from us. I remember looking out the back window of our car. They made those other people get out of their car. They were Negroes. And although we were Catholic, which they hated, they hated Negroes more. I only remember the man — the driver. There were others in the car but I looked away when they were getting out. I think there were women — several women. And maybe another man. But at that point, the men

176

with the torches yelled at my father that we should go. They yelled something nasty I didn't understand, but it was clear we should leave. And my father, he drove away as fast as he could."

"What happened to the people — the Negro people?" Priscilla asked.

"Well, I don't know," Jackie said, her voice rising. "I was a child. I never found out. I'm not sure it's possible to find out. I asked my father when I was a teenager. I had become a little . . . rebellious. I asked him one night and he got angry. He said, 'Don't ever mention that again.' I was so upset, I called my friend Ginny and walked to her house to sleep over. But we snuck out. To the Cocoanut Grove."

Plain Jane groaned and Robbie-Lee shook his head. Priscilla shut her eyes tightly.

"I need a cigarette," Jackie said. "Right away. Where's my darn purse?"

"I brought everything in from the car; it's around here somewhere." Robbie-Lee seemed happy to have something to do. He found Jackie's purse and handed it to her. She rifled through it until she found her cigs and lighter.

"I'm sorry, Mrs. Bailey White, I should have asked you first if I could smoke," Jackie said. She was definitely starting to sound like her old self again.

"Not at all," said Mrs. Bailey White. "My husband used to smoke Camels." At the mention of her husband, the rest of us glanced at the mantel. "I may as well tell you," she added, "I didn't actually kill him."

"Huh?" This from Robbie-Lee.

"Well, I've been waiting a long time to tell the truth of what happened, and now seems as good a time as any," she said. "Does anyone want to hear it?"

"By all means," said Plain Jane. I, for one, was not so sure.

"But you went to prison," Robbie-Lee said. "You were found guilty."

"Aw, that doesn't mean a doggone thing," she replied dismissively. "I was guilty, but not of killing him. I was guilty of being unfaithful." With a touch of anger in her voice, she added, "I suppose y'all find that hard to believe. Hard to believe I was ever young. Or beautiful. Or unhappily married, so I had an affair."

"Wow," said Jackie between puffs.

"I was married young, against my wishes. My daddy said I had no choice — I had to marry the son of his business partner. Nobody knew I was in love already, and if they had, they'd have skinned me alive, because my boyfriend was, well, he was not a white man."

"Well, then, what was he?" This was Jackie.

"He was . . . colored."

Priscilla leaned forward to look at Mrs. Bailey White closely, as if to convince herself that those words really had come from the older lady's mouth.

"I knew him all my life. His name was Benjamin. One day when I thought my husband had gone into town, Benjamin and I were dancing. That's all we were doing — dancing. But my husband came home early and I didn't hear him on account of the Victrola. I'm sure you can guess his reaction." Mrs. Bailey White sighed before continuing. "It happened very fast. My husband pulled out a gun and shot me. He got me right here." She rubbed her upper arm. "Benjamin charged at him and they wrestled for the gun. I heard the gun go off and I thought Benjamin was shot. Then I realized it was my husband. Benjamin had accidentally shot him right through the heart."

"Lordy, Lordy," I said under my breath.

"Benjamin made a bandage out of a towel and tied it tight to stop the bleeding from my arm. I told him to leave — to get going. He looked sad, but he knew I was right. He'd be hanged without a trial. At least I would have a chance.

"We said our good-byes and he promised he'd come back for me when the time was right, when things were all smoothed over. But I was convicted. I was sent to jail. And I never heard from Benjamin. I told myself he would have written or visited if he could. Sometimes I even lied to myself that he was waiting for me somewhere, maybe up north."

"You never heard anything?" Plain Jane asked gently. "Not even through his family or friends?"

"I heard a rumor he went to Chicago or maybe Detroit. Not much to go on. After all these years, I doubt he's even alive. Or if he is, he probably has a family."

"I don't understand why you were convicted," Jackie said. "Didn't you claim self-defense? And what about your arm? You had a gunshot wound to your arm! Couldn't you have just claimed there'd been an intruder?"

"I was afraid to mention there'd been anyone else here. I just said that Wilford — that was my husband's name — he came home and was yelling at me for no good reason. We had a fight and he shot me. I took the gun from him and shot him square in the chest. That was my story."

"And the jury didn't accept that?" Jackie said. "Why not? With a good lawyer you should have been convicted of manslaughter, not murder."

Mrs. Bailey White stared at Jackie. "You forget," she said, "this was a long time ago. A man could do whatever he wanted to his wife. And remember — women weren't allowed to serve on a jury. The jury was all men — needless to say, all white — and some of them had been friends of Wilford's! I think they set out to make an example of me. They couldn't let a wife get away with something like this. So it wasn't fair, no. But that's what happened. I'm just lucky I didn't hang. I would have, except my sentence was commuted to life in prison. I'm not even sure why. Then, last year, the parole board said I could go home. Said I'd been a model prisoner.

"You know, I'm embarrassed to admit it, but I think I actually hoped, maybe even expected, that Benjamin would be waiting for me. Not outside the prison, of course, but here at home. It was in the papers when they let me out. And somehow I just hoped he would know. That someone would tell him or send him the clipping.

"So now you know my story. And I'm lucky — lucky to have a home to come back to. This was my childhood home. I was born in this house. My father gave it to Wilford and me as a wedding gift. And this is where Wilford died, and now he's up there on the mantel. If the house had been in Wilford's name, they would have taken it from me when I went to jail. But Daddy never got around to changing the deed to my name and Wilford's. Daddy passed while I was in prison, and I inherited the house.

"It's the only good thing that's happened to me." She blew her nose into her handkerchief. "Well, at least now you know I'm no murderer. Yes, I know the things people say about me — all kinds of things. That I ambushed my husband with a shotgun. That I poisoned his oatmeal. But it's not true."

"You should write your life story," Plain Jane said suddenly. "I mean the true story."

"Oh Lord, the world ain't ready for that yet," she replied with a laugh.

"You gals are tough as a buzzard's talons," Robbie-Lee said. "You and Jackie — I can't believe what y'all have been through." He fell silent and then added, "You know, I have something I could say — about myself, I mean. Something I never told anyone." Our heads swiveled in his direction. *Now what?* I thought. He seemed to be gathering his courage, inspired by Jackie and Mrs. Bailey White but still afraid to speak up.

"I don't quite know how to say this, so

I'm just going to say it," he said finally. "You all may find this hard to believe, but I . . . I . . . I am . . . I am a —" He choked on the words. He tried again. "I am a —" But he couldn't go on.

We waited while he coughed and fidgeted. "This is very hard for me," he said. "But the truth is I am a h-h-h-h —" he stuttered. He tried again. The best he could do was, "I am a home."

"You're a what?" asked Mrs. Bailey White.

"I'm a homo —" he said, louder now but still unable to finish the word. This was agonizing to watch. Taking one more deep breath, he blurted out, "I am a homosexual."

This was the most amazing nonnews the rest of us had ever heard. Jackie closed her eyes, and I swear she was trying not to smile. "Well, of course you are, Robbie-Lee," she said sweetly. "We already knew that."

"Oh my God!" he howled. "You mean it's *obvious*?"

"Well, probably not to everyone," said Plain Jane.

"Aw, what the heck, what difference does it make, anyway?" This was Mrs. Bailey White. "I mean, you are who you are."

"But I didn't think anyone *knew*." The

183

man loved to help ladies with their home decorating projects, ordering chintz from Sears by the yard. He didn't hunt or fish, swear, go to football games, drink beer, or chew tobacco. Not only that, he belonged to the Collier County Women's Literary Society. Just who did he think he was fooling?

Only himself, apparently. He began to cry.

"Oh, please don't cry, Robbie-Lee." This from Priscilla. "We are all God's children."

Suddenly he stopped weeping, a thought having entered his mind. "Wait a second! Y'all knew all this time — and you still love me? I mean, you let me be part of your group?"

"Of course we love you, Robbie-Lee," Jackie said. And Robbie-Lee started crying all over again. We waited until he was all cried out. After a decent interval, Jackie piped up, "Well, I have some news I'd like to share. Would anyone like to hear it? It's good news. About Priscilla."

Priscilla looked up, baffled.

"Oh dear, where is it?" Jackie said to herself. She rummaged through the pockets of her skirt until she found a small envelope that had been carefully folded in half. It was now curved, having molded itself to the shape of Jackie's hip these last few hours.

"Thank God I didn't lose it," she said under her breath. For the first time since we entered the house, she stood up from her chair. Leaning across the fancy coffee table, she handed it with a flourish to Priscilla.

"What is it?" Priscilla looked totally confused.

"Just read it," Jackie said.

"It's from Bethune-Cookman College," Priscilla said, her eyes wide. She carefully removed the letter from the envelope. The letter was addressed to Jackie. " 'Dear Mrs. Hart,' " Priscilla read in a voice that was barely audible.

"Louder," said Mrs. Bailey White.

" 'Dear Mrs. Hart,' " Priscilla began again, only a tad louder but turning slightly so Mrs. Bailey White was more likely to hear. " 'Thank you for sending the application on behalf of Miss Priscilla Harmon. We are delighted that you brought her to our attention. We believe she is a worthy candidate for admission to Bethune-Cookman College. She has been accepted into the Class of 1967. Based on the essays she wrote, and that you were kind enough to send to us, the English Department has decided to offer her a full scholarship.' "

Robbie-Lee and Plain Jane gasped. Jackie was smiling but looking anxiously at Priscilla, who let the letter fall to her lap. While she was reading aloud, I noticed her voice had gotten softer and softer.

"What did she say? What is happening?" Mrs. Bailey White had missed the gist of the letter entirely.

Plain Jane turned to Mrs. Bailey White and declared, "Priscilla is going to college!"

Priscilla began to shake visibly, sobbing.

"The letter came yesterday," said Jackie. "I was going to give it to you tonight when we dropped you off at your grandmother's. I thought you might want to show it to her first." Jackie's voice trailed off.

Priscilla covered her face with her hands. She made what seemed like an effort to pull herself together, sitting up straight and wiping the tears from her cheeks.

"Thank you," Priscilla said to Jackie. She seemed to be gulping for air as she added, "I can't believe you did this for me."

"She didn't know?" Robbie-Lee asked Jackie. "I mean, you didn't even discuss this with her?"

"I urged her to apply but she kept putting it off," Jackie said. "So I called Bethune-Cookman and told them about her, how she loved to read, how she dreamed about college, and they sent me an application."

Robbie-Lee shook his head in admiration.

"That's what I like about you, Jackie. Some people say they're going to do something, but you actually do it."

But Jackie looked worried. "Priscilla, maybe I should have handled this differently. Are you all right?"

"Well," Priscilla began, "it's just that I never thought in my wildest dreams that I would ever go to college."

"But you talked about it all the time!" Jackie said. "It was your goal!"

"Not really," Priscilla said.

"Not really?" Jackie sounded alarmed now.

"It's hard to explain," Priscilla said a little defensively.

Plain Jane piped up. "This is a lot to take in. It's perfectly understandable. Especially after the day we've all had."

Priscilla looked uncomfortable. "It's not that," she said. "It's that I never truly believed I would get to go." She looked just on the verge of crying again.

"Well, you don't have to go." This from Plain Jane. Jackie shot her a look. This was not going as planned.

"There's something else," Priscilla said, dropping her face back into her hands. Then she started wailing as loud as Robbie-Lee had, minutes before.

"What? What is it?" Jackie asked, speaking

for all of us.

Priscilla looked up, and this time she let her gaze linger on Jackie's face.

I wanted to comfort or reassure Priscilla, but since I didn't understand why she was upset, I had no idea what to say. I tried out several phrases in my head and rejected them all. It was Mrs. Bailey White who knew what to do. She left the room and returned with a shawl — mohair, or perhaps angora, in a pale yellow plaid. I don't usually get excited over such things, but even I said something like, "Oh, that's lovely." Mrs. Bailey White's arthritic hands, gnarly as an old wisteria vine, slowly draped the shawl around Priscilla's neck and shoulders. Priscilla closed her eyes. She either fell asleep or pretended to. Either way, it was clear we'd hear no more about the topic. Not that night and maybe not ever.

FIFTEEN

Priscilla's reaction to what should have been good news left us all even more on edge. It was Plain Jane who finally broke the spell.

"My dear," Plain Jane said to Priscilla, whose eyes fluttered open, "you don't have to surrender your dreams forever."

I looked at Plain Jane as if she'd lost her mind. Only ten minutes or so had gone by, and anyone could see that Priscilla wanted to be left alone.

"What I mean to say," Plain Jane added, "is that I'm a gray-haired lady. And I just had a lifelong dream come true."

This was a welcome change of course. "My first book of poetry has been accepted by a publisher," Plain Jane said proudly.

After a round of congratulations, Robbie-Lee said, "But I thought you'd been publishing your poetry all along. Isn't that how you've been making a living?"

"Alas," Plain Jane replied, "one cannot

make a living writing poetry. Unless you happen to be Robert Frost."

So the question lingered in the air — how *did* she make a living?

Plain Jane saw that we were hoping she'd reveal something, for once, about herself. "The truth is," she began nervously, "well, the truth is that I pay my bills by writing for magazines."

"You mean like *Ladies' Home Journal* and *Good Housekeeping*?" Mrs. Bailey White sounded impressed.

Plain Jane glanced at Jackie. "No, more like *Sophisticated Woman* and *Playboy*. I write about sex."

We could not have been more stunned than if she'd just announced she was a Russian spy and was taking us all hostage. "Well, I don't write under my own name," Plain Jane added hastily. "And I don't want people to know. Especially now that I'm finally getting my first book of poetry published."

"Golly," said Robbie-Lee.

"So anyway, Priscilla," Plain Jane said, "sometimes life has a way of fooling you. Sometimes things work out. Just differently than you expected. But that doesn't mean you have to give up your dream forever."

It was a nice sentiment, but it didn't do

much to cheer up Priscilla, who had slid down so far into the sofa cushions, she looked like a child. We were delaying the inevitable — that some decisions had to be made. How long should we stay at Mrs. Bailey White's? What now? Then again, maybe Priscilla had the right idea. I let my head sink into my chair, hoping for a short, healing sleep.

"Wait a minute, Dora," Jackie said. "Everyone has told something about themselves tonight except you."

I lifted my head and scowled at her. "There's nothing to tell."

This was greeted with an undercurrent of grumbling around the room. "I'm just boring old me," I protested. To myself I was thinking, *I have never fired a gun at anyone and gone to prison. I did not escape from an historic nightclub fire. My mother was a nurse, not a stripper turned alligator hunter.* Even Plain Jane had been living a more exciting life than I had — writing sexy stories on the sly for magazines in New York and Hollywood. The only thing that made me special was my turtles, and everyone knew about that already.

"Oh no, you're not getting away with that 'boring old me' stuff," Robbie-Lee said crossly.

"Why don't you tell us about your marriage?" This was Plain Jane, coaxing and gentle. "How long were you married? What happened?"

I felt angry. Cornered. Just because they had all spilled their guts, did that mean I had to too?

"There's nothing to tell," I repeated, but the tears that rushed to my eyes betrayed my true feelings. Everyone waited while I collected myself. "Aw, heck, my life is just not that interesting," I said, wishing I didn't sound so defensive. "Me and Darryl, we grew up together. We were best friends. We went steady in high school. We got married. And it didn't work out."

This was sort of the Cliffs Notes version of my life, and my friends glared at me, willing me to say more.

"Well," I continued, "when we were growing up, we were together all the time. His mama used to say we were like Siamese twins. He lived next door. Maybe that was all there was to it — he lived next door and there was no one else our age to play with. Neither of us had brothers or sisters."

I was warming up now. "When we were kids — I'm talking eight or nine years old — we would climb this wonderful tree near Lee Street. You had to follow a little path around some palmetto bushes. The tree was made for us. I couldn't even tell you what kind of tree, but there were layers of sturdy branches close together, mostly on one side. One thick branch made up most of the other side, as if the trunk had split in two, decades before. I suppose it was hopelessly lopsided, but to us, the tree was perfect.

"It wasn't the tallest tree around, but something about the way it was situated, on a bit of a rise, meant you could see the whole town from up there. Not that there was much to see, but it put everything in perspective. On one side of us were the Everglades, a canopy of trees that spread to the edge of the horizon. To us, the Everglades were as majestic as any mountain range — not that we'd ever seen any actual mountains other than in books. In the other direction — and just as endless, or so we thought — was the Gulf, sparkling like a million diamonds but always changing colors, depending on the clouds. The Gulf connected us to magical places — the Keys, Mexico, and the Caribbean Islands. Both the Everglades and the Gulf were beautiful from a distance but full of danger. This was our world. We didn't know any other.

"We started to think of it as 'our' tree. I always climbed straight to the top because I thought I could touch heaven from there. Darryl was different. He would take his time, trying different routes, exploring the shape of the tree. I should have realized then how different we were. My dreams were big, and I wanted to get there fast. Darryl enjoyed the journey. He didn't even care if he got there.

"Now all he cares about is money. Maybe he never had any real dreams. Maybe he didn't want to touch the sky, or see the world beyond the Gulf and the Everglades.

"But I remember one day when I think he did. We were at the top of the tree. Darryl was talking about how the train sounded louder from up there than on the ground. 'You know what?' I interrupted him. 'This is what it must be like to be on a boat out at sea.'

" 'What? You mean like out on the Gulf?'

" 'No, I mean anywhere. The Gulf, the ocean. This tree — our tree — it's like a sailing ship. Like the *Nina,* the *Pinta,* and the *Santa Maria.*' Darryl warmed to the idea. He said, 'We should be looking for pirates! You never know when you're going to run into pirates.'

" 'Ahoy, mateys,' I called out. 'Grab the jib! Lower the sails!' I couldn't remember any more sailing terms from the books my mama had read to me, like *Robinson Crusoe* and *Treasure Island.*

"And so we played there, on the branches of our secret tree, lost in time and place. The trunk of our tree had become the mast of a great schooner; its branches became billowing white sails. We were attacked by pirates brandishing swords. We were shipwrecked on deserted islands. We were homesick and seasick and incredibly, deliriously happy.

"It was," I added, "the best day of my life."

I had never had that thought before. I thought I sounded silly, and I peered from face to face to see the reaction of my little group of friends. I didn't know any of them a few months earlier, and now they were the custodians of my deepest feelings. I felt raw and exposed until I realized that they were all, in fact, crying.

"You are a natural storyteller, Dora," Jackie said softly. "You can take a simple story, like climbing trees with Darryl, and turn it into poetry."

"It is a form of poetry," Plain Jane said. She grinned. "See — you have a talent. And you didn't even know it. Maybe you should find out where it comes from."

So I was a born storyteller. And in that instant, I knew they were right. How strange to be almost thirty years old and not realize I possessed this talent until my friends pointed it out to me — on one of the scariest nights of our lives, no less.

Then Plain Jane turned to Jackie. With a hint of mischief in her voice, she asked, "Jackie dear, isn't there something else you'd like to tell us — about yourself, I mean?"

"Why, whatever do you mean?" Jackie replied in a deliberately casual voice.

Something was up, but no one felt like pursuing the hint.

"Another time, then, Jackie," Plain Jane said. But Jackie just smiled.

Sixteen

We must have all fallen asleep, or something close to sleep, because next thing I knew I was awakened by snoring. Robbie-Lee and Mrs. Bailey White seemed to be in some kind of competition over who could make the most god-awful racket I'd ever heard. I've always reacted badly to being awakened suddenly. I was feeling mighty cranky when I saw something — or someone — out of the corner of my eye.

Just a shadow. But then the shadow moved. Over by the back door.

I breathed in so sharply, my rib cage hurt. I tried to scream but all I could do was squawk like a startled chicken. Still, it served the purpose by waking everyone up — even the snoring duo. The commotion that followed would have been comical under different circumstances.

The fireplace was providing only a dull glow. Several of us flailed about looking for a lamp or light switch. Mrs. Bailey White improved the situation slightly by turning on an old Tiffany-style lamp with a very low-wattage bulb, just enough to turn the shadow into a full-fledged apparition.

"What do you want?" Mrs. Bailey White yelled in the direction of the intruder.

"Holy cow! It's Dolores!" shouted a very surprised Robbie-Lee.

I don't know what stunned me more — that Robbie-Lee's mother was there or that she was dressed like a man. A pair of rubber boots came up past her knees and a fly-fisherman's vest tried but failed to contain her bosom.

"I came here to tell y'all you're in a whole lot of trouble, especially you," she said, pointing at Jackie.

"How did you get into my house?" Mrs. Bailey White demanded.

"That door in back," Dolores said with a shrug. "You could've at least locked it."

"But how did you *get* here?" This from Plain Jane. She meant, I guess, that Dolores didn't have a car and Mrs. Bailey White's house was too far to walk.

Dolores's leathery face was easy to read. She pursed her lips and rolled her eyes. "In my boat, of course!" she said. "There's a new channel — oh, 'bout eight foot wide."

With pride she added, "Cleared most of it myself."

I was wondering what kind of boat could be navigated through a path so narrow. A canoe, of course, but then I remembered that Dolores made a living hunting alligators. A flat-bottomed rowboat would do the job. It also explained the clothing.

"But how did you know we were here — at this house?" This was Robbie-Lee again, but his question was, I'm sure, one we all wanted answered.

"I heard tell what happened tonight," Dolores said. "Word spreads fast around here, you know. I figured y'all came here. Where else were you going to hide out?" She said the last two words mockingly.

"We're not hiding out, we're collecting ourselves and trying to figure out what to do." This was me, and I admit that I sounded a tad defensive.

Dolores laughed. "Y'all don't know nothing about life," she said with such disgust, I thought she might spit on the floor for emphasis. "You're damn — what's the word? — naïve. They are all looking for you and it's only a matter of time before they come here."

"Holy shit," said Mrs. Bailey White, surprising us all with the cuss word. "I'm on parole. I'm going to end up back in jail."

"Not if she" — and Dolores pointed again at Jackie — "faces the music."

"I guess they recognized the car," Jackie said quietly.

"Of course they recognized the damn car," Dolores replied. "They know it's yours. But the rest of you" — she swept her hand through the air — "y'all might be able to keep out of trouble."

I felt a small jolt of hope rise in my chest. Maybe there was a way to get out of this after all. What we needed right now was leadership. And if that leadership came from a retired stripper turned alligator hunter, so be it. When you're in trouble, you can't afford to be picky. You don't need Mr. Right to change your flat tire when you're stuck on the side of the road. Any man will do.

Dolores did not disappoint. "Robbie-Lee, you come home with me," she said. "You stay here," she said, pointing at Mrs. Bailey White, "and act like you never left." Dolores turned her authoritative gaze on Priscilla. "Lord have mercy, no one can ever know you were there. You should hide out here until dawn. Then walk to Mrs. B's house — it can't be more than a half mile. Just scoot on out to the road and act like you're walking to work. Don't let anyone see you come out of this driveway, though." Dolores took a closer look at Priscilla and added, "And you've got to clean yourself up. Fix up your hair. Iron those clothes. You're a wrinkled mess and no one will believe you're going straight to work from your grandma's house looking like that.

"As for you," Dolores snarled at Jackie, "you'll have to take these two gals home" — she meant Plain Jane and me — "and hope to God no one sees you. If you wait until a few minutes after six, you'll be fine."

"Why six?" Jackie asked meekly.

" 'Cause that's when the sheriff and the other boys meet at the Fish House for breakfast."

"And then I should just continue on home, leave my car in the driveway, and go inside?" Jackie looked forlorn.

"After you drop the other two off, and not right in front of their houses either. Let them walk partway so they aren't seen with you. Or the car."

"And then what?" Jackie sounded like Marie Antoinette on her way to the guillotine.

"They'll come get you. You'll have some explaining to do. But at least this way you can protect your friends."

"Of course, of course," Jackie murmured.

"Now, wait a minute, wouldn't it be better if one of us, at least, said we was there? So we could be a witness for Jackie's side of things?" This was Robbie-Lee, ever the chivalrous gentleman.

"That's a bad idea," Dolores said quickly. "That won't help her one bit."

"Excuse me, Dolores," Jackie spoke up softly. "Is there any way we can find out what may have happened? I mean to the community, Priscilla's community. Was anyone . . . killed?"

Priscilla sobbed into Mrs. Bailey White's shoulder.

"I don't know," Dolores said. "I know the church is gone. And the tent — the revival tent. Don't know what else."

"Terrible. Just terrible." This was Jackie, sort of to herself.

"Aren't you going to ask about the people you tried to mow down?" Dolores asked Jackie. Her bluntness made me wonder whose side she was on — ours or the Klan. "Don't you know you hit one or two of those men?"

"I didn't see any 'men,' " Jackie snapped back, sounding more like herself. "I saw some people running around with white robes and hoods over their heads. They weren't men, though. They were monsters."

"Well, you ran 'em down."

"Did I?" Jackie said. "Are any of them . . . dead?"

"Don't know that either."

Plain Jane interrupted. "I think Priscilla needs some water or something," she said, sounding alarmed.

Mrs. Bailey White scurried off toward what must've been the kitchen. When she returned, she and Plain Jane hovered over Priscilla like she was a baby bird fallen out of its nest.

"Oh my God," Jackie said suddenly, half rising from her chair. "My kids! My kids must be wondering where I am! I need to call them!"

"No phone — sorry," said Mrs. Bailey White. "Had my phone turned off years ago."

"You wouldn't be able to use it, even if she had one," Dolores said to Jackie. "That would leave a record that you were here." Dolores laughed under her breath, then added, "Look, it's already four a.m. You'll be back by six or so. You can tell 'em you had a flat tire."

"How strange." Jackie's voice was hoarse. "I'm in trouble but not the hoodlums who burned down a church and terrorized a group of citizens."

"We're not really citizens," Priscilla said.

203

She sounded stronger now that she'd had some water.

"This is a stupid world," Jackie said to no one in particular.

"Let's go, Junior," Dolores said to Robbie-Lee. "We don't gotta wait until dawn. Better if we go now."

I was sorry to see them leave — Dolores, who at least seemed to know what to do, and Robbie-Lee, our only man.

We were to leave next, and surprisingly the time passed quickly, at least for me. For Jackie, though, it may have been a very long two hours. She kept looking at her watch. Finally, it was time. We slipped out the back — Jackie, Plain Jane, and me. Priscilla would leave last, on foot, as planned.

The sound of the Buick's engine turning over was loud enough to set off a chorus of hound dogs, but they were a long way off and not too likely to call attention to us directly. Jackie had hoped to drive without headlights but had to drop the idea, thanks to fog so heavy it seemed to hang in sticky tendrils, like Spanish moss from the trees.

I did not want to go home. I'm not sure why but going to the post office seemed safer. No one would be there yet and I could use my key, go inside, and pretend everything was normal. Jackie and Plain Jane were in no mood to argue, so they dropped me off in the back parking lot of the Green Stamp Redemption Center, the cinder-block architectural wonder a few hundred yards behind the employee entrance to the post office. I felt sad, relieved, and a little sentimental as they drove away. I couldn't help but think how much had changed. Just two days before, I had spent a mindless hour inside the Green Stamp building, try-ing to decide which toaster I wanted, hav-ing waited until double stamp day to trade in my little stamp books so I could get a better deal. At the time, there was nothing more important to me in the entire world. How odd the place looked to me now, and how idiotic I'd been to care so much about a toaster. The night's events had left me feeling like a stranger in my own life.

Everything went as planned. Plain Jane was dropped off at the end of her cul-de-sac and walked the rest of the way home. This left Jackie, alone, to pull into her drive-way.

Ted was in Atlanta and the twins were asleep. But, she said later, Judd was sitting bolt upright on the living room couch like a nervous parent.

"Oh, Mom," Judd groaned in relief when he saw her. "I kept thinking I should call the police. I'm so glad you're okay." He was trying to stifle tears — and was humiliated that he was not succeeding.

"Did you?"

"What?"

"Call the police?"

"No," Judd said. "I don't know why, but something told me not to."

"I'm glad you didn't." For a fleeting second, Jackie considered Dolores's advice to tell a simple lie about a flat tire. But Jackie wasn't that kind of mom. And Judd wasn't that kind of kid.

She told him the whole story.

SEVENTEEN

We stayed away from each other — an act of self-preservation. As Mama used to say, better to be a scaredy-cat and *alive* than brave and six feet under.

Jackie stayed at home, waiting to be arrested or at least questioned at any moment. She wished Ted was home so she could talk to him, but he was on one of his trips for Mr. Toomb. She didn't dare tell Ted over the phone.

Dolores told Robbie-Lee that Priscilla's grandmother was okay but that several Negroes had been injured. Robbie-Lee whispered this information to me at the post office, where he stopped by, pretending to buy stamps.

Nothing had appeared in the paper about the church fire. I wanted to reach out to Priscilla, to see how she was doing, but I didn't want to take the chance of complicating her life further. She was, I knew, in more danger than any of us, even Jackie.

But after a full week passed, I went to look for Priscilla. I took the bus and waited for her at the stop near Mrs. B's house, hoping to catch her on her way home. I did this three times but she didn't show up. That's when I got up my nerve to walk to the house and try to talk to her there. I thought maybe she was living with Mrs. B full-time now, for some reason.

I expected Priscilla herself to answer the front door, since that seemed to be part of her duties. But my knock was answered by a much older woman, her back stooped slightly, with tight, gray curls peeking out from under her maid's cap.

I was so surprised, I took a step backward. "Where is Priscilla?"

The older woman craned her neck to look at me carefully. Her eyes were angry. Or maybe she was just plain tired from living too long and seeing too much.

"She ain't here no more." She said it in a way that let me know there was no point in asking questions. Now I wished I had dressed better. If I hadn't been wearing slacks, a polo shirt, and my Keds, I might have been able to put on airs. I could have gotten more information, maybe even wormed my way inside for a chance to speak to the Boss Lady.

But I skittered away, aware that I was probably being watched, which made me so self-conscious that I tripped on my shoelace, the one with three knots in it that always seemed to come undone at the worst possible moment. I knew what I had to do next, though. I went back to the main road and took the next bus, but only as far as the Esso station. From there I called Jackie from the pay phone.

"What?" Jackie screamed predictably. "She's not there anymore?" Within a half hour, Jackie pulled up. There was only one place to go — to Priscilla's grandmother's house. We hadn't made that journey since the night we'd encountered the Klan. I wasn't sure we'd ever have the nerve to drive that way again, but there we were, only this time it was just me and Jackie.

As we drew near the church, I felt queasy. I looked at Jackie out of the corner of my eye. She was very pale, and she was biting her bottom lip, but something about the way her hands held the steering wheel made me realize she was going to be okay.

I tried hard not to cringe at the sight of the burned-out church. It had the forlorn look of an abandoned campfire. Then I spotted one hopeful sign — a small scaffold, in what would have been the sanctuary, hinted at rebuilding if not rebirth. It brought tears to my eyes, and when I glanced at Jackie, I realized she had seen it too.

When we arrived at the bungalow community, it was still daylight. We'd only ever seen the place at night, lit up by the Buick's headlights. One very old lady sat on the porch of the first house, smoking a pipe. She turned her head slowly to stare at us, but her expression didn't change, even as we drove slowly past.

Priscilla's grandmother's house was easy to pick out because I remembered that a log-cabin quilt — red and blue — had been neatly tucked around a saggy-looking couch on the porch. Even at night, the quilt had been visible. I went to the door and knocked gently while Jackie waited in the car. There was no answer.

Just then someone called my name. It was Priscilla, walking up the road carrying a bucket of water in each hand. She set them down, right in the middle of the road, and ran to me.

"Dora! Dora!" she cried out. She hugged me so tight, she nearly squashed the life out of me. Then she ran back toward Jackie, who was getting out of the car, and threw her arms around her too.

"Come in the house!" she cried, and we obeyed. The house was so dark inside, I felt like I was falling into a well, but a few seconds later Priscilla yanked open a gingham curtain that covered the house's only window. "It's still kind of dark, isn't it?" she said apologetically. "I could light the kerosene lantern, but Grandma doesn't like to do that during the day."

"Where is your grandma?" I asked, wondering if she would really want Jackie and me in her house.

"She's still at work, picking watermelons." Priscilla gestured to a small kitchen table. "Let's sit here," she said, adding, "My great-grandpa made these stools." She brought us cups of porch-brewed tea, which we sipped politely. I remembered what my mama always told me: When you're visiting someone who's rich, by all means, look around. They probably would be disappointed if you didn't. But when you're visiting someone who's poor, keep your eyes to yourself. You don't want to make them feel bad.

"Priscilla," I said, suddenly remembering the purpose of our visit. "Where have you been? I mean, you're not working for Mrs. B anymore?"

Priscilla looked down at the table and sighed.

"What is it, Priscilla?" Jackie asked in her nurturing voice.

"Yes, what was it you couldn't tell us that night?" We all knew what I meant by *that night,* but even though I avoided the words *Klan* and *fire,* it still made the three of us shudder.

Priscilla cleared her throat. "Well, since you came all this way to see how I am, I guess I ought to tell you." She took a deep breath before adding, "I'm going to have a baby."

"You're *what?*" Jackie shrieked. *"A baby?"*

Now it was my turn to look down at the table. I was probably as shocked as Jackie but my instinct was to keep my emotions and my opinions to myself. Anyway, I knew Jackie would say enough for the two of us.

"How could you do this?" Jackie wailed. "How could you throw your future away like this?"

Priscilla seemed to think carefully before speaking. "I didn't know I had a future," she responded slowly. "I never really thought I'd find a way to go to college. And then I met someone."

"Oh my God!" Jackie said, then, "How did this happen?"

"Well, the usual way, I suppose," Priscilla replied, with an attempt at wryness.

"I meant why did you let this happen?" Jackie sounded more like a mother than a friend.

"It was just a onetime thing," Priscilla replied.

"Well, that's all it takes! One time!" Jackie said.

"It's my life," Priscilla said firmly. But after a moment, she added, "I'm sorry you went to all that trouble, getting me into college."

I was beginning to think we should leave. "Jackie, you need to calm down," I said. "Maybe Priscilla is *happy* about it."

"Oh," Jackie said. Obviously that thought had not occurred to her. "I'm sorry, Priscilla." Then she added, "So — are you? Happy about the baby, I mean?"

"Well, no, I wouldn't say I'm happy," Priscilla said softly. "I've made the biggest mistake of my life."

"How far along are you?" Jackie asked.

"Five months," Priscilla said, patting her belly. Under her loose-fitting shift, you couldn't tell. I realized this was the first time I'd ever seen her without the maid's uniform.

There was a miserable silence, like when

you're at the dentist and you're waiting for the novocaine to work. I had this sudden longing for days gone by, when my life was boring. At least my former life was predictable. I felt resentment toward Jackie, 'cause once again she had misstepped, making assumptions about the way things work here in the South. The chances of Priscilla going to college had been so small, who could blame her for not truly believing that could ever happen? Maybe Priscilla — like poor white girls too — got pregnant because she didn't have anything else to look forward to. Such girls were in the habit of letting life happen to them. How hard it must be to keep fighting for your dream when that dream is probably a mirage. Maybe, I thought, they'd learned to grab happiness for the short term. Find a lover, not a husband, because men don't stick around anyway. But a baby — now that's something, or rather someone, that lasts. Babies grow up to love you forever. You are the center of the child's universe. Maybe that's why some women allowed it to happen. How else to find perfect love?

Of course, there were women who got pregnant on purpose in order to trap a man, just to push him toward the altar. That idea had always disgusted and astonished me, because it required deceiving the person you supposedly loved most.

The thought of Priscilla trapping a man seemed especially unlikely. First, she was too nice. Second, the man was not even mentioned. Maybe she'd had a momentary lapse of judgment and had just been unlucky.

Priscilla interrupted my thoughts by asking a surprising question. Without looking either me or Jackie in the eye, she almost whispered, "Does this mean I'll have to quit the group?"

"The group? You mean our group?" Jackie looked at me, as if she was making sure she understood. "Why, of course not! It's not the pregnancy, it's the fact that you'll lose this — this great opportunity. That's why I care about it, and I'm sorry if I'm, well, if I'm making this harder on you. I just wanted you to go places in life. The way you were always talking about Zora Neale Hurston and Bethune-Cookman College and how you were going to go there someday — I was so sure that was going to happen that I helped *make* it happen." Her tone was apologetic and maybe, also, a little wistful. "I've always regretted that I didn't finish college. But you're right — it's your life. I should have stayed out of it."

"No!" Priscilla shouted with such force that Jackie and I jumped. We had never heard her sound like this before. "Please don't say that!" Then, calmer, "It was the nicest thing anyone has ever done for me. No one ever had faith in me like that! And now I've let you down, and I've let my grandma down, and I will never go to college and make something of myself." Her voice trailed off but there were no tears, just a deep, sad ache that seemed to roll off her and fill the tiny room every time she breathed.

A lost chance is hard enough, even when you're able to make peace with it over time. But watching a young woman win and then lose the lottery of life in such a short period — well, it sickened me, especially because she was so very likeable.

I figured we would never see her again. The divide between us would now be too wide. She had not only lost her chance at college, she couldn't even work for the odious Boss Lady anymore, a demeaning job but a whole lot better than working in those watermelon fields. She would always be welcome at the literary society meetings, but I knew the chances were not good that she'd get there. She'd be too exhausted.

As we drove back, Jackie and I were

slump-shouldered and too depressed to talk. The day's events had been too darn sad.

Another week passed. Jackie began to think the powers that be were going to ignore her. After all, she reasoned, how could they accuse her of anything without implicating themselves in something much more sinister? She grew confident. She grew cocky. She drove all the way to Sarasota, where she found a pay phone outside a strip mall. She called every Washington agency she could think of, with a lot of help from a long-distance operator who must have been wondering what in the name of our sweet savior was going on. Yes, she told the operator, she was aware there were branch offices of the FBI in Florida. No, she didn't want to talk to any of them. And no, she really didn't want to say where she was calling from or give her home address at this time. She wanted to reach someone in *Washington* — the FBI, the Department of Justice, even the White House. She left messages with secretaries who promised that come hell or high water, someone would call back within two hours.

She had thought that being a witness to a gathering of the KKK in which a church was torched would be a high priority. She would provide the details if someone "senior" called her back.

For two hours — and an extra fifteen minutes, just to be sure — she stood in that hot little phone booth, waiting, staring at the phone. Several times people rapped on the glass, wanting to use the phone. One man even rattled the door, but she yelled at him and leaned against the door from the inside. The booth smelled of spilled Dr Pepper and chewing gum. Would that phone ever ring?

It did not.

Jackie cried all the way home. What was it that one of the secretaries had said? "That's pretty common, ma'am, but we will get someone to talk to you and get the specifics." She pictured housewives like herself by the hundreds. Did they all call from pay phones? Were the stories similar? Did they all feel confident the authorities would do something, then realize in horror they were wrong?

She pulled up just as I was leaving the post office. "Hey," she called out, and I could see she'd been crying. We drove to my bungalow. I didn't think the whole world needed to see her all fallen apart like that.

In my hurry, I forgot about Norma Jean, my watchturtle, who lumbered toward Jackie as soon as I opened the gate, making that god-awful noise that sounded to most people like a dog barking.

"Oh my God!" Jackie screamed, grabbing my arm. "What is *that?*"

"Norma Jean, stop that!" I scolded. I crouched down and rapped lightly on her shell. She retreated into the bushes.

Jackie was still gripping my arm. "What *was* that?" she cried.

"Just a snapping turtle," I said. "Come on into the house."

The turtle encounter had shocked Jackie out of her weepy state, and over glasses of Coke, she told me what happened.

"I'm glad the FBI didn't reach you," I blurted out, almost under my breath.

"What?" Jackie's arched eyebrows rose to an incredible height. "What? How could you say that? What are you saying?"

"Look, Jackie," I said, trying to stay calm, "you do not want to mess with these people."

"These people — Klan people?"

"Yes."

"Don't you think I know that? I mean, give me some credit here, obviously I know they are *dangerous.*"

"This is going on all over the place, and it's something we have to handle ourselves."

"Meaning Southerners? Southerners have

to handle this themselves?" Jackie looked pissed.

"Yes, Southerners. We have to end this. Believe me, it doesn't help when outsiders . . ." I stopped, realizing I'd gone too far. "Look, Jackie, I just don't want you to get yourself killed. You don't know what you're dealing with."

"What a mean little redneck town this is," Jackie said bitterly. "I had no idea it would be so . . . Southern."

"Well, what did you think it was going to be like?"

"Ted told me it was a little fishing village by the sea. I don't know . . . I guess I didn't think of Florida as being like this."

I sighed. One of the most annoying things about Yankees was that they didn't know their history. They didn't understand Florida at all. "I don't know what they teach y'all in school up there in the North," I said, shaking my head. "Florida fought for the Confederacy. This was a rebel state. Matter of fact, Florida was the third state to secede, and proud of it. Jackie, what you are is a fish out of water. That's what this is all about. You're a northern fish trying to swim in a little old southern pond."

A fresh stream of tears dripped down Jackie's cheeks. I went to the kitchen and ran the hot water. I found the softest cloth I had, a handkerchief that belonged to my grandma, dampened it, and returned to Jackie. I washed her face as if she were a child. "Go on home," I told her. "Get some rest. You can't change the world all by yourself."

The following day Ted came back from his trip. The only one at home who knew the story was Judd, and Jackie knew she could count on him to stay quiet. Her plan was to wait for the right moment to tell Ted.

But Jackie was good at procrastinating, at least when putting something off suited her purposes. She told us later she'd been "gathering courage" to tell Ted but was "diverted" by other activities in town. She claimed to be involved with an upcoming event, the biggest one of the year — the annual Swamp Buggy Festival.

I didn't buy it. But then again, I had no idea what she was really up to.

EIGHTEEN

The Swamp Buggy Festival, I suppose, was our way of coping with the mud and muck of spring — similar, I guess, to some folks I read about who live in Canada and throw an ice festival in the middle of winter. You just get so sick of the snow — or in our case, mud — there's nothing left to do but throw a party.

First, I guess I need to explain that a swamp buggy is a crappy vehicle, open to the sky, that seems more truck than car. What made a swamp buggy special was the enormous balloon tires — and I do mean enormous. Usually they were airplane tires, either bought from armed services surplus stores or collected in the swamp after a plane crash. Picture a tire so big, the driver has to climb a ladder to reach the seat of the vehicle.

The racetrack was seven-eighths of a mile long. A driver could move to the head of the pack through speed and aggression, but it helped his chances if he was good at guessing the location of the deepest mud holes (which, of course, slowed you down if you hit 'em).

Surveying this scene of muddy mayhem was the local beauty selected as the Swamp Buggy Queen, perched at the top of a telephone pole so she could be at eye level with the drivers. Even so, she was splattered with mud by the end of the race. After she'd climbed aboard the winner's buggy, the two of them — hand in hand — would jump together into the mud.

To be honest with you, I never figured out why anyone would want to be the Swamp Buggy Queen, but the competition was brutal. The winner for 1963 had been announced already, with her photo on the front page of the newspaper. She was a lanky lass with a bouffant and a toothpaste-model smile. In other words, she looked pretty much like every other Swamp Buggy Queen over the years.

I couldn't imagine why Jackie would give a hoot about the Swamp Buggy Festival. At first I thought maybe one of her twins was involved in some way, maybe as one of the Swamp Buggy Queen's many attendants. But that couldn't be right. Jackie's daughters wouldn't have a chance. There was no room on the platform for girls who were new in town. Worse, Jackie's girls were from *up North.*

The Swamp Buggy Queen was supposed to be crowned in a ceremony prior to the race. Then the crowd would follow the queen and her consorts to the swamp buggy track, a half mile away.

But there was to be a new, added attraction at the ceremony this year: the radio station and the chamber of commerce had cooked up a plan to reveal the identity of Miss Dreamsville. A few swamp buggy purists were opposed to the idea, saying it would steal the thunder from their queen. But the chamber and the radio station insisted that surely the two women could share the stage gracefully.

Jackie, meanwhile, was secretly preoccupied with protecting her charade to the end. She knew she couldn't keep the secret under wraps forever. Besides, she could not have been more thrilled that her big moment would occur at the festival. There was nothing Jackie loved more than making a big splash.

The big day arrived, and Jackie had still not told Ted about the Klan. That ugly chapter in her life was beginning to seem like a bad dream. Today was her big day and she was going to enjoy every second. She had other things to think about. She was supposed to give a short acceptance speech. What should she say? And, of course, there was the question of what to wear.

She decided not to prepare a speech but to wing it. As for her clothes, this remained a vexing problem. If there was ever a time to dress up like Ava Gardner, today was the day. But sadly, Jackie came to the conclusion that she would have to play down the glamour. She needed to stay under the radar to maintain the surprise. How could she show up at the festival, supposedly just to stand in the crowd with her kids, looking spectacular? It was tragic, but ordinary clothes would have to do.

She had done her makeup and hair but was still wearing her muumuu when she saw the early-afternoon edition of the newspaper had been tossed onto the lawn. In Boston, she would make a mad dash for the newspaper in her house clothes and no one would care. But southern women didn't leave the house, *ever,* without full makeup, coiffed hair, stockings, and jewelry — what my mama used to call "the works." Jackie had marveled at the discipline this required, tried it, and given up after two weeks. She still dolled herself up, but only when she actually *went* somewhere, like the post office or the Winn-Dixie. Not to retrieve the newspaper.

She grabbed her floppy hat and sunglasses — necessities, she had learned, even for a few moments outside — and slipped on a worn-out pair of low-heeled pumps she kept by the front door. Her kids teased her all the time because she never went barefoot outdoors. Her feet were too tender, she said, and that might have been true. A more likely reason was her fear of Florida bugs.

Jackie had already learned, from personal experience, an important rule of southern life: be cautious about picking up anything that's been laying on your lawn, even if it's only been there for a minute. There were all kinds of scary stories, most of them true, about spiders, wasps, and even snakes crawling into the folds of a rolled-up newspaper. That is why Jackie had acquired the habit of holding the newspaper away from her body and shaking it ferociously before carrying it into the house. She was so caught up in this ritual that she didn't hear a car pull up a few feet away. When she glanced up, she recognized Mr. Toomb's personal town car, a black Lincoln with a mirror finish. The driver was a Mr. Hendry, usually called just Jim. He motioned for her to come closer and rolled down the electric-powered window. It was the only car in town to have this much-coveted gadget until Jackie bought the Buick.

"Miz Hart," he called to her, "I need you to come with me."

"Why?" she asked, almost dropping the paper. "What's wrong? Has something happened to Ted at work?"

"No, ma'am, at least I don't believe so. Mr. Toomb say he just want to talk to you for a few minutes. Just a coupla minutes."

"Talk to me?" Jackie later said she found this very strange. "Hasn't he ever heard of a telephone?"

The chauffeur shrugged. Jackie leaned into the car. "Gad, it must be hot wearing that uniform," she said. "But listen — I can't come with you. I have things to do! And I'm not dressed properly."

"But he say it's important, and I was to come carry you over there in this here car." He looked genuinely worried.

Jackie too was worried. Or at least wary. She had never been to Mr. Toomb's house. Few people had.

"Looka here, it only take a few minutes of yo' time," pleaded the long-suffering Mr.

Hendry. Only when the thought occurred to Jackie that the elderly chauffeur might get into hot water if he returned without her did she start to cave in.

"Could I just change quick?"

Mr. Hendry looked at his watch. "No, ma'am, he's already waiting," he said grimly.

"Well, I have to get my keys and my cigarettes!" Jackie nearly yelled. She stomped to the house and returned seconds later. "This is crazy," she said, opening the back door and climbing in. "I'm only doing this for you, Jim — Mr. Hendry. I know Mr. Toomb's a mean man to work for. But just so you know, I'm not in the habit of allowing myself to be kidnapped."

"Yes, ma'am." He did a quick three-point turn using the neighbor's driveway.

Jackie fumed most of the way there. "I've finally been invited to the place, and look at me! Just look at me! I'm wearing this stupid muumuu and my ugly shoes." At least, she thought to herself, she had been wearing lipstick already.

"So . . . do you know what this is all about?" Jackie asked as they neared the gate to the property.

"I don't know, ma'am, he don't confide in me."

The gate opened by some sort of remote

control onto a private road. Jackie forgot her annoyance the second the house popped into view. As she'd heard tell, the Toomb mansion was a precise copy of Twelve Oaks, the palatial home of the Wilkes family in *Gone with the Wind.* Still, she was shocked to see it in person, and couldn't resist the temptation to hum a few bars of the theme song, with Mr. Hendry glancing at her in the rearview mirror.

They pulled up under an overhang that was more decorative than useful. Before Jackie had time to think, Mr. Hendry had moved around the back of the car and opened her door.

Jackie wanted a cigarette in the worst way. She had missed her chance, though, because Mr. Hendry waved her toward the house. "You'd best be going in there right now," he said.

The massive front doors to the mansion seemed to open from the inside by themselves. She was greeted by a butler dressed like a Confederate soldier. "Follow me, Mrs. Hart," the man said in an accent that was hard for Jackie to place. She nodded, determined to remain composed.

The butler motioned for her to follow. They climbed a long, curved staircase that made Jackie wish she was wearing a ball gown, just so she could have swooshed back down those stairs — Scarlett O'Hara style — on her way out. She peered down over the railing. A maid was placing palm fronds, one at a time, in a vase so large Judd could have hidden inside.

Judd, she thought. *Maybe this has something to do with Judd.* The only other time she had encountered Mr. Toomb was at the jail where poor Judd was being held on account of his having learned Russian.

At the top of the nearly endless staircase, Jackie felt light-headed. She was hungry, thirsty, and in desperate need of a cigarette. Hopefully, this meeting would not take more than five minutes or so, and Mr. Hendry could take her back home to finish getting ready for the festival.

The butler gestured toward a set of double doors. He knocked lightly, then ushered Jackie into the most beautifully appointed office she had ever seen. Directly in front of her, about thirty feet away, was Mr. Toomb, sitting behind a desk fit for a king, which indeed he was — in Collier County.

"Mrs. Hart," he said, "please come in and sit down." Jackie, who was trying very hard not to seem impressed, sashayed forward like a model on a Paris runway. She knew she looked terrible, she told us later. But she was not going to let him have the upper hand.

She was so fixated on making the right impression that she didn't notice another person in the room until she was nearly to the empty chair where she assumed she was supposed to sit, opposite Mr. Toomb's desk. It was Ted, leaning on the sill of a window to the left of Mr. Toomb.

"Ted!" she said, and was even more startled that he didn't respond or even turn to look at her.

"Mrs. Hart," Mr. Toomb began, as Jackie — now completely rattled — sat down slowly, never taking her eyes off Ted. "Mrs. Hart," the old man began again, "I believe we have met before — at the police station, when the sheriff thought your son was a Russian spy. Do you remember that day?"

"Why, yes," Jackie replied, finally wrenching her eyes away from Ted and back to Mr. Toomb. "How could I ever forget?"

"And of course," Mr. Toomb continued, "your husband here is one of my most valued employees." Ted continued to look out the window.

"Mrs. Hart, let me be frank with you," Mr. Toomb said.

Jackie finally found her voice. "By all means," she said, folding her hands to hide the fact that they were trembling.

"Well, Mrs. Hart, I am aware of what happened."

"And what was that, Mr. Toomb?"

"An incident involving your car."

"My car?"

"Several weeks ago, you attempted to run down several of our most esteemed local citizens, who were attempting to put out a fire at a church south of town."

Jackie closed her eyes. She felt nauseous. "Esteemed local citizens?" she said bitterly. "Putting out a fire at a church south of town?"

A little sarcasm can be a good thing, but as Mama used to say, it's like cooking with pepper — a little goes a long way. Jackie had begun to understand only recently that she came on too strong. She realized that in the South, keeping your temper in check trumped everything else.

"Mr. Toomb," she said, having collected herself by studying the grain in the wood of his magnificent desk, "I believe there has been a misunderstanding."

"A misunderstanding?" Mr. Toomb sounded doubtful. Ted, finally, glanced at Jackie.

"Yes, you see, Mr. Toomb, that is not what happened at all."

"Well, then, what did happen, Mrs. Hart? Because in our neck of the woods, you can't run down innocent men with your car. You actually hit one of those men, didn't you know that, Mrs. Hart? Fortunately, his friends took him to the hospital, and he survived."

Jackie swallowed hard. She glanced at Ted but he was staring out the window again. "Mr. Toomb," she said, no longer able to bite her tongue, "this is what I saw — a bunch of men wearing white sheets, with holes for their eyes so they could see. Several of them were carrying torches. They weren't putting out the fire. They had started it."

Mr. Toomb slammed his hand on the desk. "Mrs. Hart, I have kept the sheriff from arresting you these past three weeks. I brought you here today because I wanted to give you a chance to apologize. One word from you, and this ends right now. I know the man you hit, and I've discussed this with him. He is willing to let it go for the sake of peace in the community."

Jackie didn't answer him. "May I smoke?" she said instead.

"Well, yes, of course," Mr. Toomb said.

They sat there on opposite sides of the desk, with Ted still standing by the window, only now he was leaning harder on the sill, his head bowed and almost touching the glass.

"So what have you decided, Mrs. Hart? Will you apologize?"

"No!" Ted said suddenly in a sharp voice. He turned to face them both, standing up straight, the way he used to look, Jackie thought, in his Army uniform. "This is too much to ask, Mr. Toomb. I won't let you ask my wife to sell her soul. I love her for who she is, and I wouldn't want her any other way."

His words sucked the air out of the room. Jackie beamed and tried to suppress the urge to gloat. Mr. Toomb would not meet her gaze but just shook his head.

"Well, then," the old man said wearily. "You'll have to expect the sheriff and his boys will confiscate your car and take you in for questioning." He drummed his fingers on the desk. "What is it," he added suddenly, "with you Yankees, anyway? When y'all come down here, you get all high and mighty, shaming us for our way of life, for something you don't even understand. We are good Christian people."

Maybe she was caught off guard and thinking the worst was over, but Jackie snapped. "Good Christian people don't

234

burn down a church," she almost yelled. "They don't terrorize people."

"Ha! Terrorize people! What do y'all think you did? I mean Sherman's March and all that? Y'all wrecked the South. You didn't have to do that. Y'all think you're so much better. Ha! Don't forget — you had slavery too, even in Massachusetts."

"This is absurd!" Jackie screamed. "Yes, we had slavery in the North, but you know what? We ended it back in the seventeen hundreds! And it didn't take a war to do it! The people decided slavery was wrong and passed laws to end it!"

"You think things are so much better for Negroes in the North?" Mr. Toomb was shouting now. "From what I hear, your schools are just as segregated — your neighborhoods, your churches."

"We never claimed to be perfect!" Jackie was standing now and pointing a finger at Mr. Toomb, something which had probably never happened in his long life. "There are plenty of bigots in Boston, New York, Chicago . . . plenty! I know that!"

Ted moved away from the window. He slipped behind Jackie and put his hands on her shoulders, trying to calm her down. It didn't work.

"You know what year this is, Mr. Toomb?"

Jackie said, unstoppable now. "This is nineteen sixty-three! Nineteen sixty-three! This is not *eighteen* sixty-three. The Civil War is over. The world is changing whether you like it or not, Mr. Toomb. And in many different ways."

The veins in Mr. Toomb's neck and forehead were showing through his crepe-paper skin. "I think you two should sit down for a minute and collect yourselves," Ted scolded. They complied. Jackie lit another cigarette and puffed away furiously. Ted poured a glass of water from a crystal pitcher and gave it to Mr. Toomb.

A full five minutes passed. The storm appeared to be over when Mr. Toomb suddenly looked at his watch and slapped his hand against his forehead. "Oh gosh darn it, I am supposed to be over at the Swamp Buggy Festival. It starts in less than half an hour."

"Well, I'm sure they'll wait for you, Mr. Toomb," Ted said kindly.

"Oh, yes, the Swamp Buggy Festival," Jackie said. "Oh dear, we should be getting over there too. Our children will be waiting for us."

"Well, I suppose I can give you a ride," Mr. Toomb said, automatically going into southern gentleman mode. He sounded worn down, exhausted. "We wouldn't want your children to be worried about you."

Mr. Toomb made a quick phone call to Mr. Hendry. "Jim, I'm leaving for the festival right now, and I'll have two guests with me in the car."

"Mr. Toomb?" Jackie asked sweetly, in that kind of voice that disarms men as quickly as your brain freezes when you eat ice cream too fast. "I was just thinking — could you ask the sheriff to wait until after the festival to question me? I promise I'll go straight home and I'll meet him there. But I wouldn't want anything to take away from the festival."

"Excellent idea," Mr. Toomb said. "I'll make that clear." He made another call while they waited.

"What exactly is it that you do at the festival?" Jackie asked as they hurried down the stairs.

"I'm the master of ceremonies," he replied, just as they reached the bottom of the stairs. "After the mayor gives a speech, I get to introduce the new Swamp Buggy Queen. And this year — that Miss Dreamsville woman, whoever she is. I get to announce her too. It's sort of like the Oscars. They'll hand me an envelope. Lots of suspense."

Jackie hoped that neither Ted nor Mr.

Toomb noticed that she squeezed her eyes shut. What a mess. But since Ted had certainly lost his job already, she reasoned it probably made no difference.

"So I am not taking Miz Hart back to her house?" Mr. Hendry asked.

"No, we're all going to the Swamp Buggy Festival," Mr. Toomb said impatiently. Mr. Hendry gave Jackie a perplexed look, then shrugged. There was some confusion about where they would sit in the car. Mr. Hendry wisely stayed out of it. Jackie seemed to think that as the only woman, she should sit between the two men in the backseat. Ted intervened, though, and insisted on sitting between her and Mr. Toomb, maybe so he could referee if things got ugly again. Mr. Toomb didn't really seem to care, as long as they got going in a hurry.

"Don't want to be late, Jim," Mr. Toomb said to Mr. Hendry, who responded by stomping on the accelerator.

"By the way, Mr. Hendry, I think Mr. Toomb should arrive at the festival by himself," Ted said. "You can drop us off a block or two away."

Mr. Toomb would never have asked. But Jackie noticed he didn't object either.

In short order, they were at the edge of town. At Ted's suggestion, Mr. Hendry dropped off Ted and Jackie at the Dairy Queen. They could walk the rest of the way to the festival from there.

As the car pulled away, Jackie could think of two appealing alternatives: hitchhike to Boston or go into the Dairy Queen and order the biggest chocolate sundae known to mankind. How she had looked forward to this day, and now it was in ruins. She was in trouble with the law for the first time in her life. She had caused her husband — who had just stuck his neck out for her — to lose his job. On top of it all, she wouldn't even get to savor the announcement that she was Miss Dreamsville, since she was either going to be a no-show or appear in her muumuu and ugly shoes, which was not exactly what she'd had in mind.

"Come on," Ted said. "We may as well go see what this damned swamp buggy thing is all about. We can tell our friends about it when we move back north."

"Are you sure you want to be seen with me?" Jackie asked, trying to be funny.

He put out his arm for her to hold and she took it as if they were on a date and going for a stroll.

Unfortunately, Jackie and Ted didn't know that the worst place they could ask to be dropped off was near the Dairy Queen, since the recent spring rains had left a layer of extrathick mud along the aptly named Lake Drive. Worse, some kind of tiny, hopping creatures were swarming the area — lime-green frogs, not more than a half inch in length. Trying not to step on the little critters while avoiding the deeper mud holes made for some tricky walking. Jackie was screeching, clinging to Ted. As Mama used to say, all you can do in a situation like that is laugh, which is exactly what they did.

But when they got close enough to Fifth Avenue to see the crowd starting to assemble, it didn't seem funny anymore. "We should just go home," said Ted. "Look at me. Look at my suit." Ted's expensive Florsheim shoes were encased in mud the color of mocha frosting. The same clotted mess clung to the hems of his pant legs. Jackie's bare legs were filthy, and the mud had worked its way inside her shoes. She could feel it squishing between her toes.

"We look like refugees," Jackie said.

"I don't want to be seen like this," Ted muttered. "Let's go home."

Jackie hesitated. Now that she had seen the size of the crowd, and the jerry-rigged platform someone had constructed earlier in the day, she wanted to be up there.

"What about the kids?" she said. "We said

240

we'd meet them there."

"Like *this?*"

"Well, we don't have time to go home and change. We can just say we had car trouble. I think it would look worse to Mr. Toomb if we didn't show up at all."

This line of thinking appealed to Ted. "True," he said, "but I'm not sure anything will make a difference. Not after what happened today."

"Well, if it doesn't make any difference, why not go? Like you said, this may be our one and only chance to see a swamp buggy festival. Or a swamp buggy queen." She tried to sound playful and flirty.

Ted smiled. This was the fun side of Jackie, and he hadn't seen much of that lately. "Okay, Jackie, you're right. But what are we going to do later?"

Jackie didn't want to think about that. "You could stay here with the kids. Or do something else to keep them away from the house. I don't want them to be there when the sheriff interviews me or takes me to the station. Or whatever." Her voice trailed off.

"But I want to be with you! I'm not letting you face this alone!" Ted pulled her closer.

"Wait, the swamp buggy race is after the opening ceremony, and the kids will want to walk there with the crowd and see that."

They were both relieved at the thought. "Ted, do I need a lawyer?" she asked softly, as if saying it too loud would make it real.

"Of course you need a lawyer. I've already been thinking of who to ask."

They walked glumly toward the crowd, which had tripled in the previous five minutes. "I didn't know there were that many people in this whole town," Ted said, surprised.

"Well, I think they come from other towns to be here. And the newspapers. See the photographers?"

"And television too! From Fort Myers," Ted exclaimed. "They have a new station there — CBS."

Television? That got her attention. She'd been thinking of a way to bow out — maybe find Bill McIntyre or Charles from the radio station, the only two people who knew. Bill was supposed to write down her real name on a slip of paper and seal it in an envelope, to be opened and read aloud by someone, and then she would dash up to the stage. She now realized the "someone" who would make the announcement was Mr. Toomb, which sent her stomach into contortions. If she could find Bill or Charles, maybe she could persuade them to postpone the Miss

Dreamsville announcement.

But to be on television? This was a temptation neither mud nor muumuu could discourage.

"Look," Ted was saying, "there's Mr. Toomb up on the platform. See those chairs? Near the microphone?"

"Ted," she said solemnly. "I want to thank you for saying what you did today — for sticking up for me with Mr. Toomb."

Ted sighed. "Jackie," he said slowly, "I should never have brought you down here."

"Oh no, don't say that." Jackie was starting to panic. Despite all the awful things that had unfolded that day, oddly enough, her marriage seemed back on track for the first time in years. But now what? Maybe the surprise of learning she was Miss Dreamsville would prove too much. She didn't want to embarrass Ted. It dawned on her that she hadn't considered his reaction at all. She'd been so mad at him, she hadn't cared. Judd, she knew, would be momentarily humiliated, but he was a survivor and would bounce back. The twins — well, she figured they hated her anyway. But her husband — how would this affect him?

"Ted," she said, as they continued walking, "did you really mean those things you said about how you love me for who I am,

243

and that you wouldn't want me any other way?"

"Of course."

They had reached the back of the crowd. The people nearest them turned and stared at their filthy clothing. "Car trouble!" Jackie said. "But we came anyway! Couldn't miss this!"

She started searching the crowd for the kids. Finally she spied Judd leaning out a second-floor window of the five-and-dime, the only two-story building in town. Judd loved the five-and-dime and spent considerable time there, along with the hardware store, which had a wonderful warped wood floor that the owner refused to fix.

You couldn't miss that red hair, just like hers. He had binoculars (only Judd would have thought to bring them), and she waved until he honed in on her and Ted. A few moments later Judd was by their side, flushed and happy.

Jackie was wondering why the twins hadn't shown up yet. Charles from the radio station was testing the microphone. Just as he said, "One, two, *three,*" the girls appeared miraculously. As soon as they got a look at their mother's clothes, though, they fled back into the crowd. The sight of Jackie in the dreaded muumuu — muddy, no less —

was beyond redemption.

Jackie was beginning to think she'd rather be with us, her faithful literary group, and started scanning the crowd. Finally, she saw Robbie-Lee and knew we'd be clustered near him — Plain Jane, Miss Lansbury, Mrs. Bailey White, and me. We were all there except Priscilla, who couldn't attend since she was Negro.

Meanwhile, *we* were on the lookout for *Jackie.* Plain Jane and I spied her first, standing with Ted and her kids. She did not look like she was having a good day. We waved but at that moment the ceremony began.

"Howdy, y'all!" the mayor screamed into the microphone. "This is a great day for Naples! Let me introduce our visiting dignitaries." Usually this would mean the Collier County dogcatcher and the president of the local mosquito spraying commission, but for once, some muckety-mucks had come all the way from Tallahassee. Not the governor, mind you, but the state's insurance commissioner, a man named Jonah Jones, and the top tourism official, Tyvee W. Walker III, who was as good at promoting himself (some said better) as he was the state.

Mr. Toomb was up next. He needed no

introduction, but the mayor plunged ahead, not wanting to miss an opportunity to fawn over one of our wealthiest citizens. Mr. Toomb's job, in turn, was to announce the Swamp Buggy Queen and place the crown on her head. This year's queen was a blue-eyed bottle blonde named Janey Sue Underhill. Since the queen's identity was announced beforehand in the newspaper, the event was lacking in drama. Still, we could usually count on someone in the crowd to pretend that there was, in fact, suspense. There was much cheering and applauding when the new queen appeared — Houdini-like — from behind a curtain near the back of the stage.

Sometimes the queen was nice, but I couldn't work up much enthusiasm for Janey Sue. I'd had a few encounters with her at the post office and thought she was a little too confident for someone only seventeen years old. She wasn't too bright either, and she had a relentless quality that made me want to get out of her way. Like an amoeba, one of those tiny creatures you can see under a microscope that keeps moving in circles, Janey Sue was brainless but determined to survive. While she couldn't be bothered to be polite to other females, she found her friendly side the second a

246

man walked into the room. The men didn't pick up on it but the women always did.

Surprisingly, she was wearing what appeared to be a very expensive gown. No homemade dress for this year's queen, no sir. Janey Sue wore a strapless silver concoction, either silk or satin, with sequins in all the right places. Dang, that girl looked like she'd been sewn into that dress, and maybe she had. Not wanting anyone to think — heaven forbid — that she might be trying to look sexy, she wore demure white gloves that went all the way past the elbow. Well, at least that way she saved on a manicure.

After Mr. Toomb stuck the crown on the new queen's head, she was expected to burst into tears, and Janey Sue did not disappoint. She carried on so loud that Big Bert, the half-deaf bird dog, started howling, and you could hear his flea-bitten self a whole block away. You'd think that would be enough to get her away from the microphone, but no. She had a few remarks to make first. She thanked her daddy for working a second job to pay for her dress. She thanked her mama for raising her to be a proper young lady in the southern tradition. She thanked God in heaven (twice). She thanked Mr. Toomb for no reason at all. By the time she was thanking her grammar school teachers, one by one, I was almost in a trance from studying a blade of grass that was tickling my big toe. When I finally looked up, Robbie-Lee winked at me, shrugged, and grinned. *Yeah,* he seemed to be saying, *this is corny and awful, but hey, just think how much fun we'll have talking this to death later on.* My spirits were raised too at the thought of the big surprise that was unique to this year's festival: the long-awaited introduction of our town's very own radio star, Miss Dreamsville.

But darn it all, our theatrically inclined Swamp Buggy Queen would not leave the stage. Only her parents were applauding at this point. Finally, the mayor and the chamber president corralled Janey Sue and herded her toward the back of the stage.

Just when we thought it was time for the big announcement, we realized there was one more item on the agenda: the crowning of Little Miss Swamp Buggy. This year's little princess was, surprisingly, a brunette. Going back as far as I could remember, I think they were always blond. She was a sweet-looking child who curtsied and giggled and seemed to enjoy herself despite the starchy-looking dress, pale blue tights, and patent leather shoes, which made me squirm on her behalf.

At last, with a practiced and quite charming salute, Little Miss Swamp Buggy departed from the stage. Our mayor, with the chamber president, Mr. McIntyre from the radio station, and Mr. Toomb, stepped forward, forming a semi-circle around the microphone. They looked so much like a barbershop quartet that for half a second I expected them to burst into song. There was an awkward moment while they looked at each other, unsure what was supposed to happen next. Finally, Mr. McIntyre took the lead, whether he was supposed to or not. "This is the moment we've all been waiting for!" he called out joyfully. "The best-kept secret in town!" He stepped back and gestured to Mr. Toomb.

"It is my pleasure," Mr. Toomb dragged out the words, "and an honor to announce the identity of Miss Dreamsville. No one knows who she is except Mr. McIntyre at the radio station and, of course, Miss Dreamsville herself. Mr. McIntyre, hand me the envelope, please."

Mr. McIntyre checked one pocket of his sport jacket and then another. Finally he found it — a small, cream-colored envelope — and waved it in the air triumphantly. With an exaggerated flourish, he handed it to Mr. Toomb.

The crowd surged forward, shoulder to shoulder. Thunder rumbled far away, soft and soothing like an old man talking to himself about days gone by.

Mr. Toomb adjusted his glasses. He opened the envelope slowly, using his finger as a knife. As he removed a small, thin sheet of paper from the envelope, children stood on tiptoes and adults leaned forward. But instead of reading the name aloud, as we expected, he stared at it. He wiggled his glasses around on his nose and stared again. Then he held the sheet of paper up to the sky, peering at it. But God was mischievous at just that moment and sent a little whirl of wind across the stage, maybe just to remind us who was really in charge. The thin piece of paper broke loose from Mr. Toomb's hands and fluttered delicately as if it had wings.

Someone shouted, "Grab it!" In what was surely the most athletic move he'd made in forty years, Mr. Toomb leaped into the air and snatched it, crumpling it in his hand.

A few people applauded. A few laughed, and thunder rumbled again, as if joining in.

Mr. Toomb caught his breath. He readjusted his glasses, smoothed the slip of paper, and seemed to struggle for composure. Could there have been a mistake?

Maybe the slip of paper was blank? Or had the wrong name? Then Mr. Toomb did something very surprising: he turned his back to the crowd. Yankees did things like that, and maybe poor whites down here in the South, but not a southern gentleman like Mr. Toomb. But there he was, at the center of the stage with his back to us, whispering something urgently into Mr. McIntyre's ear. "Yes," Mr. McIntyre seemed to be saying, or at least, his head was nodding up and down.

When Mr. Toomb turned his attention back to us, his face was sour as Polk County wine. Then he remembered the newspaper photographers and the television camera and managed a weak smile. The thunder spoke up again, this time more insistent. Finally, in a pinched voice, Mr. Toomb said the impossible:

"Miss Dreamsville is . . . *Mrs. Jacqueline Hart.*"

I think ten whole seconds went by, maybe longer, without a single soul able to speak. Finally a shout came from somewhere in the crowd, followed by a hearty chorus of boos and a general roar of dismay.

The teenaged boys who had fantasized that Miss Dreamsville looked something like Raquel Welch were livid. A few even shook their fists at Mr. Toomb and Mr. McIntyre on the stage. Even the thunder had to get its two cents' worth in, with a sound like a cracking whip.

I was finally able to move. The first thing I did was look at my friends to see if I'd heard right. Robbie-Lee was so stunned he was slack-jawed, which told me I had not imagined what Mr. Toomb had said. Mrs. Bailey White began tugging on my arm. "What did he say?" she asked, cupping her ear. When I leaned in to her good ear and told her, she pulled back and stared at me as if I was plumjack crazy, her head cocked like a spaniel's reacting to a bird whistle. Plain Jane's eyes were squeezed shut but Miss Lansbury was looking straight ahead, her eyes big as sand dollars. If the Gulf of Mexico had parted like the Red Sea, with a pathway for us to cross, we couldn't have been more shocked.

Then I thought, *Where is Jackie?* I looked at Robbie-Lee again and followed his gaze. She was still standing in back with Ted and her kids, or rather, Ted and Judd, the twins having left for parts unknown. Jackie looked surprisingly calm, even stoic, like she was performing the role of Joan of Arc in a local play and was taking the part too seriously. Ted looked wretched. Judd looked like he

252

might upchuck and I said a quick prayer, for his sake, that he didn't. I wished the storm would hurry up and get here, dousing us all and putting out this flame.

Mr. McIntyre stepped up to the microphone. "Miss Dreamsville, please join us on the stage," he said, his voice quavering slightly. Everyone now realized Jackie was in the crowd. Heads turned to get a look.

Jackie kissed Ted lightly on the cheek, patted Judd's shoulder, and managed to look absolutely radiant despite her bizarre attire. I couldn't imagine what had happened to cause Jackie's leaving the house dressed like that. As she moved through the crowd to the stage, people pulled back to let her pass, and she milked that moment for all it was worth. "Thank you," she said again and again, loud and deliberately pleasant. "Thank you so much." She never failed to smile, all the way to the platform.

When she reached the stage, I lost sight of her for a moment, until she reappeared on the arm of a Boy Scout who had the job of escorting her up the steps. As soon as they reached the platform, he detached himself from her. She continued the rest of the way alone, taking her time, smiling and nodding as she passed the mayor, the miscellaneous dignitaries, Bill McIntyre from the radio station, and last but not least — Mr. Toomb.

I'd have died on the spot if I'd been in her shoes. It must've been a very long walk to the center of the stage. When she reached the microphone, she took a deep breath, then exhaled.

"H-e-l-l-o, Naples," she said, using the same sultry voice that we listened to, night after night, but had never once connected to her. "It's Miss Dreamsville here."

The crowd murmured. This was her, all right.

"I know I'm not what you expected," she said, returning to her everyday voice. "I'm sorry you're disappointed. I didn't think you would be *that* disappointed. I guess I should have seen it coming."

She paused for a moment, then went on. "This is not how I hoped this day would turn out either. I mean, I didn't expect to be standing here in a muumuu with mud all over my feet.

"Okay, look at it this way," she said, trying a different approach. "When this opportunity came along to have my own radio show, it flipped a switch in me. I'm not the greatest mom. I'm not the greatest wife. I'm not even a good cook. Anna Mae" — she pointed to the mayor's wife, standing in a cluster of ladies — "you make the best key lime pie in the world. Me, I can't even make a Jell-O salad you'd want to eat. Sally — where are you? — the work you do with the Cub Scouts puts me to shame. I don't have that kind of patience. I envy you for that. But see, my point is we are all good at different things. And in my case, it's being Miss Dreamsville."

This approach seemed to be working, at least with some of the women in the crowd.

"I'm not like the rest of you," Jackie added. "I know that. I'm a Northerner. I don't fit in. I think I was looking for something to do that was just for me — you know, aside from raising kids and taking care of the house. I didn't set out to deceive you, and neither did Mr. McIntyre." She gestured toward the young radio station owner, who looked worried but nodded eagerly.

The crowd was giving her a chance. At least, I thought, they seemed to be listening. But then Jackie — being Jackie — went too far.

"Besides," Jackie continued, her voice rising noticeably. "Why *can't* a middle-aged mom be Miss Dreamsville? Why does that make people uncomfortable? I think we should ask ourselves that question."

Someone booed — very loudly.

"Well, fine," she said sharply. "I have news for you — the world is *changing.* Things are going to be better for women. We're going to have more options. Same thing for Negroes. You wait and see. *It's going to happen.* It already is! We have a Catholic president! People said that would never happen! The world is changing — for the better!"

"Amen!" roared Robbie-Lee, shocking us all but inspiring Plain Jane, Miss Lansbury, Mrs. Bailey White, and me to start clapping wildly. Others in the crowd were applauding too, and when I looked around, I saw it was Ted and Judd.

But this was dangerous ground. I just wanted Jackie to stop.

"If America is going to stay number one in the world," she continued, "then we have to put aside our differences here at home. We have to allow everyone to live up to their full potential. It's not about black versus white, Catholic versus Protestant, Southerner versus Northerner. That's just stupid! We can do better!"

"What the hell is this?" a man in overalls hollered from the middle of the crowd. *"Is this some kind of joke?"*

Jackie's shoulders slumped. Her momentum — and apparently her courage — were gone.

Seeing her hesitate, he went in for the kill. This time his voice was more than angry. It was mocking. "I asked you, lady, if this is some kind of joke. Or are *you* some kind of joke?"

I grabbed Robbie-Lee's arm. "We should do something," I said as he bent down to hear me. But someone else beat us to the punch.

"Stop!" The shout sounded like a young man, maybe a teenager. We craned our necks and saw Judd waving his arms wildly, his face almost as red as his hair. I exchanged glances and a shared thought with Plain Jane — *Now what?*

Judd charged through the crowd, head bent and elbows flying like a pissed-off whooping crane running off intruders who'd come too close to the family nest. As he reached the stage, he had so much momentum, he took the steps two at a time, then nearly crashed into the dignitaries, finally ending up at his mother's side. Grabbing the microphone, he spoke, gasping for breath but determined.

"My mother is not a joke!" he said. He took a few more breaths, then continued. "I'm proud of her! Why shouldn't she be Miss Dreamsville? She's smart and she loves music. She's beautiful — even though she's old! I love my mom! *God bless my mom!*" And then, as if he couldn't think of anything else to say, he sang out, *"God bless America!"*

There was a moment of hesitation, followed by an eruption of noise never heard at a Swamp Buggy Festival, a kind of hysterical joy and frantic applause more typical of a revival, like the one held outdoors each year at the Incorruptible Word of Faith Church and Ministry.

Judd had just hit the ball out of the park without meaning to. No Southerner can resist a public spectacle involving a declaration of undying loyalty and devotion to one's mama. Wars have been fought and men have died for the love of God and country, but in the South they ought to add "mother" to the list, and not necessarily last either. Even Mr. Toomb looked like he was going to cry. Judd was so astonished, his mouth hung open, but Jackie quickly seized the moment. She placed both arms around Judd in a maternal embrace that would have made Donna Reed proud, and produced her very best smile for the newspaper photographers, who crouched and leaped — and even shoved each other, not something we'd ever seen in these parts — while trying to get the best shot. The men in charge of the television apparatus struggled to keep up, pivoting the camera like an Army tank taking aim at its prey.

We could guess what the headline on the front page would be tomorrow, "Miss Dreamsville Revealed!" or something along those lines, no doubt in enormous typeface, the likes of which we hadn't seen since Pearl Harbor was attacked. Beneath it, no doubt, would be a second, smaller headline, "Son Defends Mother in Emotional Start to Swamp Buggy Fest."

Jackie and Judd had made a 180-degree turn in a matter of seconds. They'd been as welcome as carpetbaggers in Sherman's wake, and now they were the darlings of Naples. The chamber of commerce folks, the mayor, the dignitaries from Tallahassee, and — yes — Mr. Toomb had made a sharp reversal too and now appeared to be Miss Dreamsville's most ardent supporters, gluing themselves to her side like eager suitors competing for the prettiest girl in town.

Jackie, of course, loved every minute of this and played it to the hilt. She was glowing like a full moon or maybe even the brightest of all planets, Venus. Judd, on the other hand, struggled to follow his mother's lead, but the best he could manage was a confused smile.

I suppose that's what we must have looked

like too — the members of the Women's Literary Society, kept in the dark just like everyone else. I looked over at Ted, standing alone in the back of the crowd, and imagined that we looked as giddy and baffled as he did.

As Jackie and Judd finally prepared to leave the stage, a call went out for Ted and their two daughters to join them. Ted moved through the crowd enthusiastically, slowed only by people shaking his hand and congratulating him on his splendid wife and son, but the twins had vanished. The only person having a worse day than Jackie's twins was the Swamp Buggy Queen.

Just as Robbie-Lee said, "I need a drink," everything came to a halt. A voice rang out. "Will the Turtle Lady and the rest of the literary society please come to the front of the procession?"

So she had not forgotten us. This was the first time — and probably the last — that our motley little crew would be lauded. If only Priscilla had been there too. At this moment, at least, we were stars, caught up in Jackie's amazing constellation.

There were to be more photographs at the radio station, in front of the chamber of commerce, and at Jackie's house. This was too good for the crowd to pass up. Things like this didn't happen in Collier County very often. Matter of fact, they never did.

By the time we got to Jackie's, it was a few minutes past three o'clock. The newspaper photographers — and most of the crowd — were still caught up in the excitement, and although the television cameramen could not keep up and had returned to Fort Myers, Jackie was still playing the game for all it was worth. She even posed in her kitchen with a Jell-O salad. Then one of the photographers asked if she would pose outside, "in front of that hot rod convertible."

At first, she hedged. "Oh, so you like my convertible?" she asked, flirting with the photographer, who was maybe half her age. She hemmed and hawed and giggled, and then suddenly she seemed to get an idea. "Has anyone seen the sheriff?" she asked cutely. When we arrived, the sheriff had been standing in the driveway. We assumed his presence had something to do with crowd control.

When someone located the sheriff in the living room, Jackie marched right over, took his arm coyly, and beamed up at him as if they were on a date. Then she steered the sheriff over toward Mr. Toomb, who was a few feet away. Without hesitating, Jackie grabbed Mr. Toomb with her other arm. She was now anchored between the two men. "One more picture here, then with the car," she said, beaming. The sheriff and Mr. Toomb smiled dutifully. The sheriff, I noticed, looked a little wan.

This was — you have to admit — a brilliant move.

The house was jammed with people now headed outdoors, and the effect was that the threesome was carried on the tide and deposited in the driveway, right in front of the car. The photographers loved it. Jackie was laughing and smiling, only this time she wasn't acting. She had the sheriff and Mr. Toomb right where she wanted them. They knew they were defeated. After all, Jackie had just put Naples on the map. The chamber of commerce was already preparing a press release.

The case against Jackie was over.

Well, not quite.

"Mrs. Hart, did you know you have a crack in your windshield?" asked one of the photographers, an older fellow.

"Oh, do I?" she said. "Oh yes, that's right, I think it was a rock that was kicked up by a truck. Isn't that a shame?"

"Yes, and you'd better get that repaired right away, because it's only going to get worse," the photographer added.

I was in hearing distance of this, and the moment was excruciating. I wished Jackie would, for once in her life, just shut up.

"Sheriff? Mr. Toomb? What do you think?" she asked innocently. "Do you think it's dangerous? What should I do?"

"Um, yeah, you should have that repaired right away," the sheriff said glumly. Mr. Toomb nodded.

"Oh, thank you, gentlemen, so much for your opinion." Jackie was really icing that cake. Before she could ruin it, I stepped forward and took her by the arm with a time-honored diversion. "Jackie, you're needed in the kitchen," I said, unable to think of anything better. The sheriff and Mr. Toomb took advantage of the moment and pulled away from her — in opposite directions.

The crowd began to peel away in twos and threes. A few people were headed to the racetrack to catch the tail end of the swamp buggy race, or at least find out who won. After many hugs, the members of the Women's Literary Society left for our respective homes, leaving Jackie, Judd, and Ted to celebrate on their own and wonder where the twins were.

But thanks to the miracle of television,

the day ended with one more surprise — a big one. At the end of Walter Cronkite's *CBS Evening News,* Jackie's and Judd's smiling faces suddenly appeared for six seconds of eye-popping glory. The most famous voice in America read these lines with a smile:

"And now this from our new affiliate in Fort Myers, Florida. A middle-aged mother in a little town called Naples has been named Miss Dreamsville." Mr. Cronkite added his signature line:

"And that's the way it is."

POSTSCRIPT

We saw the bus before we heard it — the familiar shape of the Greyhound as it burst through a bank of swamp fog, the sticky morning mist so thick it dampened sound. The bus appeared to fly above the pavement, hurtling toward us, the noise of the engine absorbed by a million acres of marshland.

Five months had passed since Jackie's spectacular triumph. The Women's Literary Society was splitting up.

Three of us — Robbie-Lee, Priscilla, and me — were leaving town. Miss Lansbury had already left. She resigned from the library to study water conservation with the Osceola Indians. This was of course a stunning development. Librarians did not simply quit their jobs and run off to be with the Indians, at least, not any librarian that had ever worked in Collier County. As if this were not exciting enough, in her farewell interview in the local paper, Miss Lansbury announced that she was, in fact, an Osceola Indian. She had been passing for white. Her decision to follow her heart seemed to give permission to the rest of us to do the same.

We discovered, also, that Priscilla had joined our group at the library at the invitation of Miss Lansbury. It turned out that the principal and several teachers at the Negro high school had alerted Miss Lansbury to a student named Priscilla Harmon who had read every last book in the Negro high school's library. Miss Lansbury had quietly become Priscilla's mentor, choosing books for her and getting them to her on the sly.

Robbie-Lee headed to New York. But first he would escort Priscilla to Daytona Beach, where the fall semester at Bethune-Cookman College would start in two days. Jackie, along with Plain Jane and Mrs. Bailey White, would stay behind to help take care of Priscilla's baby.

Priscilla went to college after all.

I was going with Robbie-Lee and Priscilla as far as Tampa. My plan was to sleep in the bus station, then board a bus for Tallahassee. From there, I'd take another bus west across the Panhandle, through a sliver of Alabama, and to my destination — Mississippi.

Plain Jane, Mrs. Bailey White, and Jackie had come to see us off. As the bus came closer, I took my eyes off it to take one last look at the friends I was leaving behind and freeze the image in my mind.

I had been worried about Jackie. Being Miss Dreamsville had lost its fascination for her. After her identity was revealed, she quit the show, insisting it would never be the same. Ted, strangely enough, was not fired. In fact, in the wake of the Miss Dreamsville publicity, he had actually been promoted by Mr. Toomb.

Jackie needed a new project — and fast. But considering how often she admitted to having little or no maternal instinct, I was surprised, to say the least, when she came up with the idea to help Priscilla. For two whole weeks, Priscilla said no. She did not want to leave her baby, and besides, she thought it was too much to ask. But in the end, her grandmother convinced her to go.

The bus was now close enough for us to see the words "Tampa/Orlando" on the placard across the windshield. A surge of joy mixed with desperation ran through me from my scalp down to my toes. If for some reason that bus did not stop, I would have run out into the road and flagged it down. Come what may, I had to leave.

Robbie-Lee's presence was a comfort. He was calm and stoic in his usual Rock Hudson sort of way. Aw, heck, he looked poised and handsome no matter what. It was early September, the hottest month here in Collier County. This meant I looked like a well-used dishrag even though it was only six thirty in the morning. Robbie-Lee, on the other hand, looked damp but not wilted. I tried to read his emotions. Determined, I think. He was going to New York to become a star. Either that or an interior decorator. But another of his goals was to find a doctor who didn't sneer at his mother's health problem — her painful breasts. His dream was to bring Dolores north and see to it that she got the help she needed. I had no doubt he would be successful in whatever career he pursued. I was confident, also, that he would find the right doctors. But I wondered if Dolores would go along with his plan.

That part he had not considered, Robbie-Lee being one of those "I'll cross that bridge when I come to it" types. There had been a time when I would have thought he was foolish not to have every detail worked out — to be sure Dolores would agree before he went to all this trouble — but now I could see the genius in allowing the future to evolve. You could create momentum. You could launch something and see where it goes. You couldn't line everything up, like so many dominoes, and make everything fall into place.

I was proud that I had finally begun to understand this. There was no greater proof than my own plan, which was not really a plan at all — just go see where my mother had come from. To visit Mississippi. Maybe even meet Eudora Welty.

When I asked for a leave of absence at the post office, in the blank space for return date I had written "unknown." If Marty couldn't hold my job open, so be it. The only thing I worried about was my turtles, but then Judd Hart offered to take care of 'em and I had total faith in him. I was ready to take some chances and see the world, not hide behind the post office counter for the rest of my life. I didn't want my epitaph to be "She Played It Safe."

I was the first one at the bus stop, as if the 6:35 a.m. Greyhound to Tampa was my one and only chance to get out of town, even though that old bus stopped in the very same spot every single day of the year. I was beyond ready.

Priscilla, on the other hand, did not look ready at all. She was clutching her beat-up suitcase with both hands, like she was afraid to let go. Now, as the bus came close, she dropped the suitcase to the ground.

She turned to Jackie, Mrs. Bailey White, and Plain Jane. She hugged each one and, in a voice way higher than usual, pleaded, "Take good care of her!"

"Of course we will!" Jackie cried. "And remember, your grandma is in charge! She'll be the boss."

Plain Jane stepped forward at that moment and tried to turn Priscilla back toward Robbie-Lee and me. "Now, don't be sad, you'll come home often. Go on and study hard!" she said sternly.

But it was Mrs. Bailey White who calmed Priscilla down. She scooted around to Priscilla's other side, took her hand, and whispered something into her ear. It was magic. Priscilla straightened her shoulders, wiped away her tears, and managed a brave little smile.

The bus was going too fast. For three or four long seconds, I thought it would pass us by, but sure enough the brakes shrieked and it skidded to a stop, the driver having forgotten that sand piled up on this section of the Tamiami Trail. The door popped open like a secret passageway into a tunnel. The time for good-byes was gone.

Robbie-Lee tossed our suitcases on board, then took Priscilla's hand and helped her up the first, deep step as if she was Princess Grace. God, you had to love that man. He helped me next, making me feel like a goddess too, and then he hopped on himself. There was barely a second to spare before the driver clamped the doors shut behind us.

"Go to the back," the driver barked at Priscilla. She did as she was told and we joined her, breaking the rules about Negroes and whites sitting together. The bus driver turned around in his seat and gave us a bug-eyed scowl. I guess he was too tired to pursue it, and since there was no one else on board to make a fuss, he didn't stop us.

The back row was actually one long bench seat, and we half fell onto it as the bus took off. I told myself I would not look back, but I couldn't resist joining Robbie-Lee and Priscilla, turned sideways and half kneeling so they could peer out the back window.

Plain Jane and Mrs. Bailey White were waving like they were seeing us off to war. But Jackie — where was she? Had she left already? Maybe, I thought, she's jealous. The fact that three of us were leaving may have rubbed it in that she was stuck there.

Then I realized I was wrong. Jackie was in a hurry to pick up the baby, that's all. Priscilla's grandmother had to be at work by seven o'clock on the dot or lose a week's pay. For once in my life, I stopped myself from reading too much into a situation.

I was thrilled for Priscilla, who had named her baby Jacqueline Dreamsville Eudora Harmon. This was a lovely gesture, but privately I wasn't sure Naples could handle another Jackie. Apparently neither was Priscilla. Within hours of the baby's birth, Priscilla chose the perfect nickname. From that moment on, the child was called Dream.

And that is how three white ladies became nannies to a baby who was black, which — I guarantee — was a first for Collier County. Naturally, this decision resulted in some sensational fireworks. But that is another story for another day.

Thanks to the Collier County Women's Literary Society, we all found our place in the world. Jackie, Plain Jane, and Mrs. Bailey White not only took care of Dream while Priscilla was at college, they started an integrated preschool and home for unwed mothers at Mrs. Bailey White's old Victorian house. Robbie-Lee encountered some bumps in his path, but in the end, he made it to Broadway. Miss Lansbury became an environmental activist who devoted her life to our beloved Everglades. Priscilla not only finished college, she followed in the footsteps of her hero, Zora Neale Hurston, by becoming an anthropologist and a writer.

As for me, to my absolute amazement, I became a famous author and storyteller. Mine was a circuitous path — with some peculiar adventures along the way — but I wouldn't change a thing. I saw the world beyond Florida. I even lived in other states. But when I got old, a funny thing happened. I wanted to come home to Collier County. I guess I always knew that one day, I'd return to my little cottage by the Gulf.

ACKNOWLEDGMENTS

This story is fiction. It was inspired by my mother-in-law, Jacqueline B. Hearth (1928–2004), who really did create a radio show called *Miss Dreamsville* in Naples, Florida. While my husband, Blair, and his family inspired this novel, the story, actions, and characterizations are my creation.

Judd Hart is loosely based on Blair. All other characters are invented. Mr. Toomb, for example, is a composite of many people I have known, as is the sheriff. Janey Sue Underhill is my imagined interpretation of what the 1963 Swamp Buggy Queen might have been like. Any similarity to real people is coincidental.

A special thank-you to Blair for putting up with this entire enterprise. He is not only a great husband, he is a good sport for allowing me to interview him repeatedly for details that greatly contribute to the richness and spirit of this novel. Giving me his class ring — Naples High School Class of 1968 — was a playful gesture, and I enjoyed wearing it for inspiration while creating this book. (The ring has a tiny engraving of a swamp buggy on one side and a fishing pier on the other.)

I am grateful to my parents, Dorothy and Lee H. Hill Jr., for too many things to state here, although I will mention just one. Thank you, Mom and Dad, for moving us all to South Carolina in 1965, when I was six years old. No experience could have helped me understand our country more than living in the Deep South during that era. And with the assistance of my first-grade teacher, the late Mrs. Emma Long, I learned, in no time, to understand and speak "Southern."

The origins of my career (and much of the material for this book) stem from my early adulthood in Florida in the 1980s. I attended the University of Tampa, graduating with a BA in creative writing in 1982. Among many meaningful experiences was an internship in investigative reporting at *Tampa Magazine.* Later, as a staff reporter at the *Daytona Beach News-Journal,* I met Blair by interviewing him for a story. My ties to Florida continue through my alma mater, old friends, and close relatives living in Hillsborough and Pinellas counties.

While this is my debut novel, it is not my first published book. I am the author or coauthor of seven nonfiction books, including the 1993 *New York Times* bestseller turned Broadway play *Having Our Say: The Delany Sisters' First 100 Years.* I wish to thank my literary agent, Mel Berger at William Morris Endeavor, who supported my decision to try my hand at fiction and has celebrated with me the fact that I took the leap and landed on my feet. I am extremely fortunate that the visionary publisher Judith Curr and the brilliant editor Malaika Adero fell in love with this novel instantly and have been its champions from day one.

I must thank John R. Firestone, my friend and attorney, for his enthusiasm not just for this project, but for the adventure of publishing. His knowledge and love of books is an inspiration.

I wrote this novel without telling anyone, except Blair, who was the first to read it. The second was my dear friend, the author Audrey Glassman Vernick, whose insight and encouragement gave me a lift when I needed it most, and gave me the courage to complete the book.

My local writers' group (of which Audrey is a member) is owed a debt of gratitude for (among other things) getting me out of the house and away from my desk during the solitary process of writing this novel. Thank you to Audrey, Sharon, Pat, Lillian, Nina, Denise, Caren, Janet, Gwen, Kristen, and Joanne (and emeritus members Kris and Jo).

Details about Naples are accurate in most instances. By design, there were times when I changed a detail here or there to make my story flow. For example, the bus that takes the threesome out of town on their grand adventures would have stopped at a small bus station in downtown Naples. For symbolic purposes, I wanted the characters to be waiting on US Highway 41, the Tamiami Trail, heading north.

Readers may ask about the Klan as described in this novel. While the violent encounter springs from my imagination, such incidents were not uncommon in Florida in the early 1960s. I based it on interviews and research I conducted as a reporter in the state in the 1980s, as well as Blair's own recollections about Collier County. As for Jackie's encounter with the Klan on Long Island in the 1920s, readers may be surprised to learn that the Klan existed in many parts of the North as well as the South. One of those who survived a

Klan encounter circa 1925 — on Long Island, in fact — was the late Dr. Bessie Delany. The incident she described to me is included in our book *Having Our Say: The Delany Sisters' First 100 Years,* on page 139.

One last note: I have one thing in common with Dora, the narrator of this novel. As a girl living in South Carolina, I rescued turtles trying to cross a road across the causeway next to our lakeside home. (Apologies to my mother, who was kept in the dark about this particular hobby. And, in a nod to public safety, don't even think about doing this today, please, unless you have professional training.) Some were snapping turtles and too heavy (and too mean) to carry, so I chased them with a broom or stick to make sure they got safely to the other side. My childhood friend Alison was my conspirator and backup turtle rescue person. (Apologies to her mother too.) I carried on our tradition later, while living in Florida.

And I still rescue turtles today, wherever I am.

■ ■ ■ ■

Miss Dreamsville
and the Collier
County Women's
Literary Society

Amy Hill Hearth

A READERS CLUB GUIDE

■ ■ ■ ■

INTRODUCTION

When Boston-bred Jackie Hart sweeps into sleepy Collier County like a late-afternoon storm on the Gulf, young divorcée Dora has a feeling her life is about to change. Jackie immediately forms the Collier County Women's Literary Society, and, for the first time in her life, Dora feels she has found her place in the world. The 1960s is a time of shifting perspectives and dramatic change, and as these changes creep slowly into Collier County, Dora and her small group of misfit friends band together — helping each other hold onto their dreams and struggle through the complexities and hardships of everyday life united.

QUESTIONS AND
TOPICS FOR DISCUSSION

1. Discuss the various forms of prejudice that each character is subjected to

throughout the novel. Consider not only the racism that exists in Collier County but also the less overt discrimination — like the doctors' attitude toward Robbie-Lee's mother's chest pain, or the way Dora is treated for being divorced. Do you think such attitudes are inherent or learned?

2. How much of a person's character is shaped by the times in which they live? Was it difficult for you to imagine a time when segregation was so prevalent that even someone as good-natured as Dora would try "not to stare at the colored girl"? (page 19)

3. What was your reaction when Jane reveals to Jackie that she completely fabricates her sex advice articles? Did you find it ironic that she "sounded annoyed" when Jackie asked her if she had actually *done* what was written in the article? (page 62) How easy do you think it is to ignore the possible consequences of our actions when we are separated from actually having to see the results — by distance, or otherwise?

4. Dora says about Jackie, "She was, clearly, a 'Boston Girl' through and through. Cultured. Progressive. All that Yankee stuff we Southerners find so irritating." (page

17) Later Jackie says, "What a mean little redneck town this is. I had no idea it would be so . . . Southern." (page 220) How did you react to this hidden conflict between North and South? Do you think this sentiment still exists today? What do the rest of the literary society learn from Jackie and her Northern family (and vice versa) that changes these attitudes over the course of the novel?

5. Some authors (e.g., Mark Twain) intentionally use colorful storytellers who are to be believed more because of the underlying truth embedded in the story than adherence to rigid standards of objective reporting. Dora, a self-described storyteller, seems to belong in this time-honored category. Do you think she is telling the truth as she knows it? Can a storyteller be an objective narrator? Can *anyone* truly be an objective narrator?

6. What makes Jackie the ideal friend to each member of the Literary Society? What common ground do they share? Do you have someone who has been a similar presence in your life?

7. Were there any historical facts about life in Florida during the 1960s that surprised you? In what ways does fiction provide a means for a fuller understanding of a

nonfiction truth?

8. Why do you think Jackie was the only one who had such a strong response to *The Feminine Mystique*? Do you agree with Priscilla that the issues explored in the book weren't about women universally? What about Robbie's feeling that men were equally limited in their choices? Do you think their points still hold true?

9. Discuss the members' reactions to *Their Eyes Were Watching God.* What did you think of their conversation? Was anyone's opinion unexpected? Do you think their conversation was worlds apart from the discussion that would take place today when reading the same book?

10. Many characters in the book have an alter ego of sorts: Dora is the Turtle Lady, Jackie is Miss Dreamsville, Jane is Jocelyn Winston, and even Miss Lansbury is an Osceola Indian who has been "passing for white." (page 266) What do these alter egos imply about each character's personality?

11. The town is shocked and angry when they discover Jackie is Miss Dreamsville. Do you think their reaction is warranted? What does it say about the disconnect between fantasy and reality? Do you think there is a real person who could've satis-

fied people's various visions of Miss Dreamsville? Or would they have been disappointed no matter what?

12. Jackie says, "Maybe freedom means defining yourself any way you want to be." (page 159) Do you agree? How do you feel about Jane's reaction that "we are a long way from that happening"? Do you think the society members end up defining themselves how they want to be, and thus finding their freedom? Whose life do you think was changed the most by being a member of the society?

13. Dora reflects, "How hard it must be to keep fighting for your dream when that dream is probably a mirage." (page 214) What do you think is the difference between a dream and a mirage? Discuss the role dreams play throughout the novel. Were you surprised to discover Priscilla is pregnant when she seems to have the most focused dream of going to college and becoming an English teacher?

14. After everything that's happened to them, Dora thinks, ". . . now I could see the genius in allowing the future to evolve. You could create momentum. You could launch something and see where it goes. You couldn't line everything up, like so many dominoes, and make everything fall

into place." (page 269) Do you agree or disagree with her? What was your reaction to the ending? Did the protagonists follow the paths you thought they would?

15. What differences (or similarities!) did you notice between the literary society in the novel and your own book club?

ENHANCE YOUR BOOK CLUB

1. Visit Amy Hill Hearth's website at www.amyhillhearth.com to learn more about the author and to read her essay "Why I Write."

2. Each character in *Miss Dreamsville* is searching for a purpose to keep them going or a dream to follow. Bring something to your book club that represents a personal passion and turn the meeting into show-and-tell.

3. Pick one of the books that the Collier County Literary Society reads, such as *Silent Spring, Breakfast at Tiffany's, Their Eyes Were Watching God, The Feminine Mystique,* or *Little Women* to read and discuss at your next book club meeting. How does your discussion compare to the Collier County Women's Literary Society's discussion?

4. If you were to have your own radio personality name what would it be? Go

around the group and share your imagined on-air pseudonym!

The employees of Thorndike Press hope you have enjoyed this Large Print book. All our Thorndike, Wheeler, and Kennebec Large Print titles are designed for easy reading, and all our books are made to last. Other Thorndike Press Large Print books are available at your library, through selected bookstores, or directly from us.

For information about titles, please call:
(800) 223-1244

or visit our Web site at:
http://gale.cengage.com/thorndike

To share your comments, please write:
Publisher
Thorndike Press
10 Water St., Suite 310
Waterville, ME 04901